STEPS

**A DYSTOPIAN ALTERNATE REALITY:
THE IMPOSSIBLE POSITION OF BEING.**

STEPS

A NOVEL

SAM A.D.

atmosphere press

© 2024 Samantha Dagott (Sam A.D.)

Published by Atmosphere Press

Cover design by Matthew Fielder

No part of this book may be reproduced without permission from the author except in brief quotations and in reviews. This is a work of fiction, and any resemblance to real places, persons, or events is entirely coincidental.

The 'steps' concept and SLT devices remain copyrighted as an original idea.

Atmospherepress.com

To Paul, my close friends and family who buoyed me through this journey. My gratitude is endless.
And to those who have their own story to tell, go forth without hesitation.

Preface
THE ANNOUNCEMENT

Finally, it has arrived. The time of year everybody has been waiting for. The air is thick with anticipation. There is a new life, a buzz in the city. People have a skip in their...movement. You can feel the energy, like a bolt of lightning has hit, charging the population with life. The one time in the year people regain a sense of hope. The one time the population comes together. It's time for the annual Sunshine City Lottery!

It's an interesting observational time. Everyone gets to see how everyone else makes the best of their situation. What suits their physicality, their lifestyle, their needs. What adaptations or contraptions they have made to aid them. There are some real smarts and creativity among them. Some of the solutions people come up with are amazing. Especially those with a scientific or engineering background. Necessity being the mother of invention, even simple solutions can give you options. Simply watching the parade of people go by can be a real eye-opener, inspiring even.

There are very few who won't make it to the biggest event on the calendar. You've got to be there to claim your prize. And everyone lives in hope that each year it will be them.

The annual lotto date has been announced.

SAM A.D.

*

The lotto was introduced after mandatory SLTs (Step Longevity Trackers) were bought in. This new ability to watch your life disappear before your eyes via the step countdown on your wrist was not for everyone. It was a big shift for everyone to be monitored all the time. To adjust to having a limit. Due to environmental initiatives, cars had been outlawed decades ago, leaving no options to get around this conundrum. The step limit has been set at 60 000 000 steps, or around 40 years, give or take, depending what you choose.

A fair amount of people chose suicide, unable to deal with the new way. Some folks just slipped into a deep depression, never to come out. It sent the population spiralling down a lot quicker than anticipated. Not many people had sex, it was too risky now. It would trip their SLTs.

S.H.I.T. did not think about the whole sex thing and how it could be affected. Reproduction slowed right down. The population plummeted. Something needed to be done.

While the whole program was about keeping the population in check, we had swung too far the other way. If it kept going on this trend there would be no next generation to pass on knowledge, to teach to exist as human beings. More like human has-beens. The human cycle would fall out of orbit and eventually become non-existent.

Which is funny in a way, the very program that was meant to save us and control the population is the very same program that almost killed us off!

So, the lotto was started to increase happiness and general well-being. To give people something to look forward to, a reason to keep going. A highlight in their otherwise monotonous existence. And it worked. Everyone has lotto fever. Everyone wants a piece of it.

There's a special bonus draw this year, another chance for longevity and a little bit of power.

The usual random draws are:
- 500 people will win unlimited steps, to use how they wish.
- 1000 people will win the right to unmetered sex, with their SLTs paused for one hour. No contraceptives allowed. (Purely for breeding purposes, although most still enjoy the act as well).

Bonus draw:
- One lucky person will be gifted unlimited steps and an invitation to join the Step Handling and Integration Team, affectionately known as S.H.I.T.

S.H.I.T. oversaw the distribution of steps. And the lottery. It controlled and policed anything that involved steps and the SLTs. It made the big decisions for the 'good' and 'well-being' of the general population. It is a very powerful organisation. Maybe a bit too powerful. Because with power comes corruption, and egos. The usual side-effects and drama.

Anyway, enough about S.H.I.T. Back to the event.

This year the stadium will be bigger than ever before. It is anticipated that 94% of the city's population will attend. The 13-year anniversary will bring with it a huge light/drone display. And another massive drawcard, the free dance.

Everyone in attendance will have their SLTs paused for one hour of dancing. People have been too scared to dance for a long time now, despite their wants. It's going to be interesting.

Now the race to the stadium has started. This year isn't going to be easy access. Just a day ago finished an almighty storm that raged for three days and two nights. It is bedlam out there.

If you like a challenge, I guess you could call it an obstacle course.

Chapter 1
AGNES

24 YEARS, 147CM, 55KG. ROLLER.

Traversing across the park was usually a relatively easy task, sometimes even fun. Agnes enjoyed the challenge it presented. Usually, she would roll. Like a log down a hill. Except there was no hill, she was always self-propelled, but she could get to the other side, no problem. Her abs hard like giant overcooked nuggets from a lifetime of rolling.

The trade-off was her body, constantly covered in scratches and bruises. Usually nothing to worry about, just little nicks here and there. She would laugh at herself afterwards. Looking in the mirror, a scarecrow often returned her gaze, sticks, and leaves trapped in her hair and clothes. A natural ghillie suit. Therefore, she always smelled like grass and soil. Earthy.

She had become quite advanced in the art of rolling. But some unplanned unpleasant things still happened, like the times she rolled over a poo mound or two. Some things are unavoidable when you travel at ground level. It's a small price to pay.

But today is different. It had been atrocious weather last week. Persistent rain, hail, thunder, and gale-force winds reduced the usually even, rolling parkland into a minefield of mud, potholes, fallen branches, and debris. Surveying the area, she realises she has no chance of rolling the entire way today. She checks her SLT strapped to her wrist. 31 011 241 steps left. She has done well throughout her life, conserving her steps. Rolling worked well for her. She can do it; she will just have to walk. She doesn't want to. No one really does anymore, not in the traditional sense. Mostly crazy people and a few adventurous folks who refuse to be governed by the steps program.

However, a lifetime of rolling around has left her legs in quite a state. Unlike her abs, she has barely any muscle mass in her legs. They just kind of...dangle around. But today she will need them, and the park is quite big. She hopes they have the strength to carry her through with minimum fuss. Another problem is her legs are also quite short. It will take her twice as many steps as anyone else, she loathes the short-legged burden she was born with.

'A birth handicap,' her mother had always said. 'You won't live long on this earth,' she would say. Her mother was such a downer sometimes. She could just never get past the negativity she dragged around with her. People from her time, the time before SLT, often have this attitude. Understandable, given they once lived without it. They knew a better life. No wonder they are bitter. Of course, her mother is dead now. Everybody has their own way of dealing with things and Agnes had accepted her mother's way. But moving past her death, she forged her own way, different to her mother. That's why she is a roller. Everyone must choose a way to best deal with the current circumstances.

She chose rolling. Agnes is a roller.

Now Agnes finds herself surveying the park. Swimming goggles in hand. Unseen inside her head, her brain is firing on all cylinders as she tries to navigate the easiest route. Sometimes the easiest way physically is also the filthiest. Decisions, decisions.

She cannot see anyone else around. People don't while away their day having delightful walks through the park anymore, enjoying the fresh air and sunshine. A large percentage of the population won't even help others anymore. Not if it means using their steps, therefore decreasing their lifespan. To be honest, it's become rather unfriendly. Social norms are now skewed.

Agnes has given herself more time to get to the stadium than she thinks she will need because there is always some kind of challenge she isn't expecting, a curve ball from life. Because being short with even shorter legs clearly is not punishment enough. She often wonders what she's done in a past life to be dealt a fairly crap hand in this one.

Her eyebrows crinkle and lips move as she talks silently to herself, planning out her journey through the obstacles. She begins to roll down to the first obstacle, a fallen tree. It's only about six metres away, but the ground is littered with leaves, twigs, a couple of branches, some garbage that the storm blew in, and a dinged-up letterbox. They are the things she can recognise, who knows what lies beneath them.

Agnes rolls towards the tree. It's still pretty damp, and the ground is mushy and uneven. Twigs poke into her back and torso. She's wearing her swimming goggles, something she usually takes with her when she's out and about rolling around. Among other things, they protect her eyes from mud, water, twigs, and poo.

Years of practice help her navigate successfully around the broken letterbox, but not before noticing a letter inside. Skilfully she snatches it up mid-roll, placing it in her waterproof jacket pocket as she continues.

*

Rolling…rolling…bang. Into the tree.

Using her little nuggety abs, she sits up easily. Grasping some branches, Agnes manages to get on her feet. That part isn't too hard. She walks beside the fallen tree to the exposed roots and circles around. She can see the footbridge. The usually quaint and serene creek is swollen and raging as the water trickles into it from surrounding parkland. It's a little underwater at each end, not too deep, but not rollable. The arch design of the bridge provides an island of safety and dry in the middle.

Between Agnes and the bridge are more obstacles. A shopping trolley on its side, full of debris and mud that washed into it. Some sheets of corrugated iron blown off buildings during the storm. A mess of sex toys that washed down from Sin-shine City Sex Supermarket. And a tangle of discarded unused bicycles. The up and down foot and leg motion from cycling would count as steps so not many people ride a bike unnecessarily anymore. The city is littered with them, like the canals of Amsterdam. This next stage to the bridge will require walking, not rolling.

The sun is getting higher in the sky now. The day is warming up.

In fact, it is so pleasant that if you close your eyes, still yourself, and allow the sun to be your drug, you can be transported anywhere but this rubbish tip of a park. More people will start coming out as the day wears on. Everyone will be on their way to the stadium.

Agnes begins stage two of her park crossing. Coming around the roots of the fallen tree, her eyes are charting the most direct route through the shopping trolley, bikes, bits of iron sheeting, and sex toys. She can walk but it sure doesn't come easy. Eyes on the prize, she steps away from the safety of the tree. Supported by only her weak dangly legs, she starts moving.

One…two…three…steps, all going well. Four…splat!

'Nooo! Aggh!'

A wayward tree root has managed to snag an ankle, sending Agnes tripping, limbs akimbo, into one of the many big, brown bog holes where water has pooled over the past couple of days.

'Oh wow…really? Of course this happened to me!' Agnes is frustrated, punching her fist into the bog, splattering herself with stagnant mud. It's deeper and thicker than she thought it would be. The mud holds onto her fist, it takes her some effort to get it back. More like molasses, less like muddy water. She rolls onto her back, tries to sit up.

No. Nothing happening. Tries again. Still nothing happening. She can feel her abs working.

Tries again. No. Can't move. For a moment she's confused. Did she just half paralyse herself?

The viscous bath that is the bog hole now has a suction hold on Agnes, creating a vacuum underneath her, making it impossible for her to sit up. She's lying not far from the fallen tree so she is quite well hidden, masked by the bike tangle on the other side. What's a girl to do?

Tick-tock, tick-tock, the hours sneak away.
Tick-tock, tick-tock, Agnes is here to stay.

Judging by the sun's movement, Agnes has been sucked into the bog for around two hours now. The sun has been relentless. What was once a drug to a place of serenity is now slapping her in the face with full ferocity. Luckily she still has her swimming goggles on. They are lightly tinted, helping her eyes. Distracting herself, she's focusing on the sun, directing her attention to the flares it makes bouncing off her swimming goggles from different angles. Anything to pass the time.

Unexpectedly, a long shadow comes over her from behind. She can't see what it is because she is still suctioned and cannot move her head back enough to see. At this stage, it doesn't matter what it is, the relief from shade surpasses any curiosity she harbours about the unknown.

'Oh, I see you have yourself in quite a situation. Can I help you?' says the unknown shadow of relief.
    'Great, I'm delirious already. I'm screwed.' She can't believe she got herself into this situation. She has no idea how she is going to get up.
    'Hellooo? Can you hear me?' The unknown shadow of relief again. 'You're not delirious, I'm really here.'
    The shadow steps around into her eyesight and, wow! She really must be delirious! What an amazing looking…

Chapter 2
AKSEL

27 YEARS, 198CM, 82KG. STRIDER.

Being of Nordic descent, Aksel is blessed by birth. He is one of the lucky ones with excellent genetic breeding. His parents are both tall scientists from Norway and chose each other well. Most folk now marry for genetics, but some still marry for love. Aksel's parents married for genetics. They still actually liked each other, it wasn't all bad, they just weren't in love and never were. It was more like a business transaction. Luckily for Aksel, their choices give him an advantage over many.

He is very tall with very long legs. Quite good looking too. Smooth and sleek. Tanned from all the time he spends outside. He smells fresh, like sprucy, Nordic fresh. You know, like the deodorant ads from a world ago. Oh, did the ladies love him! Not that it made much difference, no one really indulged in sex anymore for fear of tripping their SLT. But they still liked to window shop.

Physically one might describe him as an alpha male, without the superiority complex. He is a rare, genuinely nice man with a heart of gold. This new world will not bring him down. He has made his choice to be a walker, or rather, a strider. Well, genetics helped a lot in his choice, after all it would be a shame not to use what you've got. And his parents would be so upset if he did not utilise the gift of genetics they planned so well for to give him the best advantage through life. Hell, they may even disown him. They are snobs.

Aksel decided to choose the middle ground. No way was he going to become a prisoner in his own home like some did. Nor would he choose the other extreme of not caring, throwing caution to the wind, and enjoying every moment regardless of outcome. Please, he did have some sensibilities. Some structure. Some rules he has set himself. For example, he will only allow himself to look at his SLT once per day. He will not allow himself to fixate on it.

It's all about the legs with Aksel. If only you could see them. They are toned and lithe hip to toe. Like a gymnast's legs.

His torso and arms are in proportion but nowhere near the fit condition of his legs. Taking the biggest strides possible while walking is his thing. The longer the better. Although longer strides did take more time. He must be careful not to fall over while striding, it slows him down, but he covers two to four regular person's steps with one of his, so it is worth it. Biggest side effect is the peculiar gait he gained by his walking style.

It was curious to watch him walk, funny even, though no one ever laughed. Everyone knew why Aksel walked like that. The same reason Agnes rolled. The same reason why everyone behaved strangely these days. And he didn't regret it, even with a funny gait.

He chose to stride. Aksel is a strider.

*

'Hellooo. Are you OK? Can you hear me?' Aksel asks again.

Agnes blinks. Wonders if she really has gone crazy, slow-cooking herself in the sun. What is this oasis? This hallucination? She is sure that there is now a good-looking, tall man standing over her right now. With amazing legs. And he's asking if she needs help? No one helps anymore. This must be an illusion. She closes her eyes again.

'Would you like some help or not? I'm not hanging around, I've got to keep moving.'

Agnes opens her eyes again. Yep. He's still there. The unknown shadow of relief takes one gigantic step over her then outstretches his hand for her to grasp. She takes it.

With height on his side, Aksel easily yanks her out of the bog, quite ungracefully. The suction vacuum makes a loud sucking *pop* noise as she is hauled out, a verbal protest from the bog, left disappointed its victim got away before it could completely devour them.

She stands, pushes her swimming goggles up onto her head to get a good look at her saviour.

Aksel stares back. He's taking stock of her. He's not quite sure what he's looking at here. This person is absolutely covered in...stuff. A consistent overall smudge of textured brown is the base coat. A top layer of grass and twigs sticking to the mud and through her hair gives her quite the camouflage/scarecrow look. Is she undercover? A spy? In the military? Why is she in this disguise? Her face is filthy, which Aksel first thought was camouflage paint. There are a few scratches here and there, but not too bad. Since removing her swimming goggles, she has a wonderful reverse panda thing going on with her eyes. The only clean part of her body. Oh, and she smells very 'organic' to Aksel. He crinkles his nose.

'You undercover or something? That is some camouflage you are wearing, I barely noticed you on my way past,' says Aksel.

Agnes is caught off guard with the comment at first, then it dawns on her she must look like a hot mess right now. Many a time she has come home only to laugh and cry at her own reflection after being out rolling.

'Uh, oh...no. This is how I look most days,' she replies, trying desperately to hold onto a shred of dignity in front of this god-like man. Realising she sounds like a real slob with that comment, she quickly tries to back it up.

'I mean, I don't mean to. It's...it's my rolling,' she explains.

Aksel looks her up and down again, trying to understand what she is trying to say. Seeing this, Agnes quickly jumps back in and spells it out for him.

'I'm too short, my legs are too short. I'm a roller. I roll everywhere to save my steps.'

The penny drops for Aksel. He's seen rollers getting around in the past but has never actually been up close and spoken to one before. What strange, slightly stinky individuals they are.

'I'm Agnes. Thanks for helping,' she says. She is in awe of him, hypnotised by his cleanliness. She's never seen anyone so tall or handsome. And he smells forest fresh. All piney and sprucy. He is the very opposite to everything Agnes is.

'Hey, I'm Aksel. Happy to help. It only cost me three steps. I was on the way past anyway. What were you doing down there? Having a nap?'

Agnes is slightly embarrassed. You can't see her blushing through the mud and for this she is grateful.

'Not exactly.' She points to the tree roots. 'I fell over the roots and got sucked into the bog. I couldn't get out,' she explains, 'I've been in there for hours.' Aksel looks towards the bridge.

'Well, if you are on your way to the stadium, you may need help to get over the bridge. It's a bit flooded. I don't think you could roll through it.' Although he quietly thinks the bath would help. Of course, he knows she's on her way to the stadium, why else would she put herself through this?

'I'm going to continue now, if you want some help to cross the bridge come with me,' says Aksel.

So, they go. Aksel with his careful, long strides alongside Agnes' multi-step mini legs. His towering frame against her short stature. His tanned, fresh, and clean pine-scented body beside her slightly smelly bog-covered body with reverse panda eyes. Both walking awkwardly in their own gait.

As an observer it would be quite funny to see these two together. The odd couple.

With Aksel by her side, Agnes is feeling much more confident as they navigate around the shopping trolley and sheets of iron towards the bridge. But before the bridge is the swamp of sex toys, bobbing around in the flood water.

Agnes feels her cheeks blush when Aksel bends down to pick up a huge purple vibrator.

'Oh, Agnes, did you drop something?' He waggles it in her face, bops it on her nose.

'Get that off, gross! Don't touch me with it.' Blushing harder now, Agnes replies in a panicked voice. Aksel finds this amusing coming from someone already covered in filth.

'Relax, it hasn't been used,' says Aksel, pointing to a pile of soggy cardboard boxes, 'see, straight out the box.' He looks up the road. With his height advantage, where he stands he can see the purple warehouse the sex toys came from. Agnes can't. She is too short.

'The flood water must have washed them down from Sinshine City's warehouse,' he observes as he shoves it into his backpack. Agnes doesn't want to know why he needs it.

As they start to wade through the water that floods the bridge entrance, Agnes kicks the collection of colourful vibrator boats out of her path. She is already almost knee-deep while the water is just creeping up past Aksel's ankles. *Step... swoosh...step.*

'Waaa!' Agnes' feet slip out from under her and she is on her way down again, this time grabbing Aksel for support. But he sees an opportunity here, an opportunity for her to have a bath. Even if it's flood water it will still be cleaner and less smelly than Agnes. So he pretends to wobble with her, pushing her off him as he wobbles the other way, sending Agnes ungracefully into the water.

She is on her back again, flailing about. Making snow angels in the water. The water is now like a storm at sea. Crashing and splashing everywhere, upsetting the safe harbour the vibrator boats were enjoying, sending them flying in every direction.

When Aksel feels she has impersonated a washing machine for long enough, he reaches down and pulls Agnes up. She is not impressed but does look a lot cleaner. She attempts to squeeze the water from her clothing.

'Thanks for taking your time.' She's frustrated. Second fall and not even halfway across the park.

Aksel scoops her up and carries her to the dry part of the bridge. He's trying desperately not to smirk even though he is most amused by her situation.

They stop atop the bridge and stand in the sun for a few minutes, allowing Agnes to dry a little. It's quiet between them as Agnes simmers down and Aksel keeps his amusement in check. Both unsure what the tone is between them now, Agnes opens the conversation.

'Thanks,' says Agnes, 'for saving me again.' Aksel looks at her, a smirk hiding just behind his concern.

'I didn't even have to waste a step for that one. You're welcome.' They share a small smile at the absurdity of the situation.

Aksel checks his SLT. 29 003 264 opportunities left to get somewhere. It's his first and only daily check. He feels good about it.

'Look.' Aksel points to two stiltwalkers going by on the other side of the park. They are clearly well-practised. They walk in big striding steps in unison. Confident in their element. They both wear orange flowing clothes. Their faces cannot be seen as they are both wearing the biggest hats Aksel has ever seen. Yes, it is a hot day, but maybe a bit over the top. From where they are standing, the stilt walkers look like a couple of giraffes stalking through the trees. How very odd indeed.

In fact, now they have taken the time to stop and look around, they notice movement here and there. People are stirring, getting ready for tonight, making their way to the stadium.

A gaggle of body builders lope about. Looking like cartoon caricatures. Over-exaggerated upper bodies and regular from the hips down. They would usually focus 90% of their training on chest, abs, and arms. Doing just enough legs to help them get around. It is never leg day in Sunshine City.

The roller skaters are emerging. You can hear the rolling noise coming before you see them. Each push action will still trigger the SLT, they just get a lot further with each push than a step. Until they get somewhere not paved. Functional to a point. It isn't uncommon to see them with scrappy, pavement-eaten knees and elbows as they push themselves to the limit for more distance.

Woosh! Something flies past Aksel's head. Small and fast. Light in colour. He looks around confused. A bird? *Whoosh!* Another one zips by, catching Agnes' attention. This time they both see it land safely on the decking of the bridge. Agnes picks it up.

'It's a paper plane.' She holds it for Aksel to see. *Woosh!* Another close by. They turn their heads in the direction of its entrance and see someone in a window of an apartment block nearby. At least they think they see someone.

The window frame is almost solid in a way. But there is the distinct shape of a head and suspicious arm hanging out the window.

'Hey! Watch out!' Aksel is annoyed. The figure's arm raises again.

Chapter 3
DEREK

48 YEARS, HEIGHT UNKNOWN, 264KG. SITTER.

Refusing to go out, 'Fat Fuck' Derek sits in his wheelchair by the window, throwing his paper planes at the two weirdos standing on the bridge.

Well, sitting in his chair is very kind. More like around his chair. Encompassing his chair. His flesh and the chair at one together, becoming the same entity. Fat flesh oozing down all around him, over the chair's structure. In fact, his ample flesh has grown around the chair, it has been that long since he has stood up. It is now impossible for him to get out even if he wants to. He can barely get the wheels to move anymore, bits of fleshy fat flapping around often get stuck in the spokes. Who knows where he ends and the chair begins, he lost track of that years ago. Derek had been smart enough to cut a hole out the bottom of his seat a long time ago now, before he became part of the chair. At least he could wheel the chair over his industrial size mop bucket to perform the basic human task of going to the toilet. Wiping afterwards, that was impossible now. That's where the mop from the industrial size mop bucket came in.

You see, Derek had chosen a path to take under the circumstances, as everyone else had.

Derek chose to be a sitter. And it is way too late to change that now.

Even though his lard burden has weighed him down and made him terribly unwell, he has lived to over 48 years old!

But his long life has come at a cost. He never goes outside. He can't get down the steps. Lack of fresh air has given him a distinct smell of steamed dim sims (much how he looked!). Greasy, white, bed sore-plagued skin, zero muscle tone, no friends, never had sex, never known love, never experienced a lot of life. Just four walls and a wheelchair. Just his online gaming persona 'Fat Fuck 63548463'. All gamers were fat fucks, there were so many, and Derek is number 63548463.

Sure, gamers live longer than most, but one must weigh up the options. Mind the pun. What's a long life worth if you have nothing? Life would drag out even longer through boredom. It could be considered an advantage with the right mindset but as said, one must 'weigh' up their options, it was not for everyone.

He is also obsessed with checking his SLT device. Although his original band didn't fit on his wrist anymore. Which is funny, because they were made to never come off once you got one. It had broken under the strain of trying to hold onto the greasy, puffy flesh. Knowing what could happen if someone stole his data, he superglued that motherfucker right back on again. Wrapped a bit of gaffer tape over it for good measure, cutting a hole through which he could see the screen.

He checked it constantly because it reassures him he has made the right decision when he sees how many steps he has left.

So, he chose to sit. Derek is a sitter.

*

Derek looks through the window at the funny couple on the bridge. He is always highly amused by people's confused reactions when they first get buzzed by the planes. Being housebound, it's something he can do to idle the day away.

He has a greasy giggle to himself.

'Stupid fools. Look at them. Wasting away their steps. They don't deserve steps. They must want to die early, walking round like that.' Derek's muttering now. He lines them up and lets another plane go.

Chapter 4
THE INVITATION

Agnes and Aksel both see the arm move and release another plane in their direction, in a similar fashion to the way in which one would throw a dart. With purpose. As it lines up to use Aksel's face as a landing strip, he expertly snatches it mid-flight.

'Ha. Got it!' He's excited and pissed off. Looking at the design and folding of the paper plane he can tell it was well made. He is even silently impressed by how well the planes have flown. He notices there appears to be writing on one side. Opening it, they are both surprised to find an invitation to a party. The handwriting is scrawled and uneven. Childlike. It reads:

> *Hello friends.*
> *Please come to party upstairs.*

They both look to the window and see the shadowy figure's arm raise to wave at them.

Agnes is first to speak. 'This is weird. We don't even know who that is. Do we?' She looks to him with a curious expression, in case it is a friend of his.

'Yeah, it's odd alright. Maybe they just need some company. Some people don't go out much to save steps. Whoever it is, they're probably just lonely.'
Normally one will not go out of their way for anyone if it involves using their steps. They certainly don't go to parties at random peoples' places. But Agnes and Aksel are feeling good. They'd both made a new friend in each other today, perking them up from the usual humdrum daily routines. They both know too well what it's like to be lonely. And the party wasn't far.
'You know what, let's go say hello for a little while. There's two of us, if shit gets weird we can leave,' Aksel suggests. Agnes nods her answer, so they start off the bridge towards Derek's apartment.

Derek can see the two read the note and talk. It looks like they are heading his way. Excellent. He hopes they have ample steps left; he's been disappointed in the past where his effort wasn't worth the measly amount of steps his victims could offer.
'Better rustle up some special drinky-poos for these two,' he mutters to himself. After one more glance to make sure they are still coming, he turns from the window to fix some drinks. Surprised, he startles and almost drops the stack of paper plane papers. He has found someone in his apartment already, standing right behind him.
'Geez! You surprised me. How long have you been here?' Derek asks. 'Why can't you just knock like a normal person? You're always sneaking around.' He's deflecting, a little embarrassed about being jumpy and not noticing his guest enter.

Agnes and Aksel are nearing the end of the park. Aksel on maximum stride while Agnes rolls beside him. She is saving her steps for the stairwell. Aksel will have no issue there, he can take seven steps at a time, Agnes is only capable of one at a time.

Faintly at first, they can now hear trumpets and a distorted female voice over a loudhailer getting louder as it approaches. Looking in the direction of the noise they see the mayor of Sunshine City, crazy Ms Turquoise Fitzenberger. As usual, to save her steps she is being carried around on her throne by her four 'assistants' (they never live long).

Turquoise Fitzenberger had an unusual accent. She pronounced her name as 'Turk-kwoise'. Now everybody calls her 'Turk-kwoise', emphasising the kw. She always smells like geranium and smoke. Her perfectly coiffured hair looks the colour you would imagine geranium and smoke to be. Suppose you could call the colour smoanium, or geramoke.

Turquoise is announcing tonight's lottery, reminding everyone to come along. She stops at Agnes and Aksel and even though only two metres from them, continues to talk through the loudhailer at them.

'The annual lottery starts in four hours. Please come along. There's plenty of prizes and opportunities to be won. Everybody come and have some fun,' she wails.

Her voice through the loudhailer sounds more like an order or threat than an invitation.

The ruckus outside brings Derek back to the window. He sees Turquoise engaging very loudly with his two potential 'donors'.

'Damn Turk-kwoise. She is holding them up,' Derek says, more to himself than his visitor.

'Don't tell me you're up to your old tricks again, Derek.' His visitor clearly knows Derek and his modus operandi. 'We talked about this. Have you forgotten what happened last time? Also, you work for me, no time for your self-indulgent side hustle.'

'Aggh...c'mon, Elio. Just because you never have to worry about your future, doesn't mean I can't improve mine. Anyway, I planned on leaving them enough to get to the lotto tonight. If they are lucky, they will still be here tomorrow.'

Chapter 5

ELIO

18 YEARS, 173CM, 71KG. BLACK MARKET LONGEVITY DEALER & IRISH DANCER.

'You're just being greedy. We both know you're never going to use them. No one lives forever, even with all the steps in the world.' He gives Derek the once-over with his eyes, judging.

'And you, my chunky friend, you can't even walk.' Elio often insults Derek. They aren't really friends, more like acquaintances as far as Elio is concerned. Derek just happens to provide a service Elio needs, therefore Elio tolerates his stinking, wobbly mass.

Elio has never, nor would he ever, have to think about how, what, where to go, for how long, or how to get there. He does what he wants when he wants. His SLT is on maximum capacity constantly. It's the reason he's been working the black market since he was 12 years old. It's dirty work but someone's got to do it. If not him then someone else will, so why not? You know, it's a 'if you can't beat 'em, join 'em' type of situation. Whilst he hasn't joined them per se, he has beaten them.

Elio's peculiar career choice was not much of a choice, he

didn't really have an option. Suffering from restless leg syndrome since birth, he was only expected to live to 11 to 15 years.

He therefore happened to be one of the few minorities in the current circumstances who appeared 'normal' in the old-school sense of the term. Normal was a word hardly used these days because there were very few who behaved as such. Normal in that he got around just fine, thank you. Others watched in awe as he strutted around, ran, Irish danced. He wasn't Irish but he loved to show off his skills and all the chaotic steps involved. It sated his restless legs. No one could believe he would waste himself away like that, but he knew he wasn't wasting away.

Some grew suspicious of his lackadaisical life, for he was always in a constant state of celebration. Always dancing, out and about, carrying on, and partying. For one to carry on in public as he did, it attracted attention and not always good. But he had the confidence of youth and max capacity, so he simply did not care.

The blackwork gang he worked for cared. He was getting noticed and if he was getting noticed then people started questioning. And when people started questioning, the blackwork gang started pressuring. If that didn't work, they would have no choice but to silence his feet. And we are not talking about felt pads here. They would happily chop those dancing feet right off and feed them to the hogs.

So, Elio fled.

He flies solo now but he is smart. Cyber smart. He does well enough on his own. Using his learned skills to benefit himself while maintaining his charade as a regular civilian.

With a passion for Irish dancing, and the black market.

Elio is a black market longevity dealer. And an Irish dancer.

*

'So what. When I get to 50 000 000 it will be enough for me to use my steps to get fit. You'll see.' Derek shifts uneasily in his wheelchair, eyes to the floor in a flush of shame. He hated when Elio did this but accepted it anyway. He was in love with Elio, but Elio could never know. Elio would put an end to their working relationship if he ever found out. Derek knew deep down Elio wasn't there to spend time with him. He just wanted his tech savviness to help his business. He was using him. But he was determined to get fit one day and impress him. Derek just needed lots of steps to begin the long road of exercising for weight loss.

His eyes crept up from the floor and lingered on Elio, his back to Derek as he looks out at Derek's potential victims walking away from Fitzenberger. They are coming their way, the tall one points up to their window when the one rolling on the ground stops.

'How strange,' is all Elio can think to say about them. His left leg has started twitching.

'Well, I thought we could do some work this afternoon, but I see your newfound friends are on their way up. I will come see you tomorrow after the lottery.' He's trying to keep his legs still, but the jittering is non-compromising.

Elio turns on his heels and quickly leaves. He does not want to be seen by Derek's new friends.

Derek's eyes latch onto Elio's retreating figure until he is out of sight, disappearing down the stairwell before the party invitees arrive. One day he will like me, Derek thinks to himself.

'I'll show you, Elio, one day I'll be fit,' he says not for Elio's benefit, more to reassure himself.

Chapter 6
FOREVER27

Legs twitching, Elio wrestles with his restless leg syndrome as he walks down the street.

'Time for a dance, eh.' He is looking down at his legs, talking to them.

Of course, there is going to be the big free dance tonight, but Elio needs some movement soon. His legs fight against his calm demeanour.

He decides to go to the one place where people never judge you or think you're crazy if you dance excessively. A place he really likes, despite everyone around him dying when he is there. A place he's been admiring someone for a while. He hopes she hasn't expired yet.

Forever27.

Forever27 is open every day/night from 2pm to 8am. It is the most notorious day/nightclub in Sunshine City. The club is also known as Suicide City, Forever Fucked, or 27toHeaven. It's where all the cool kids go. People with more liberal views on life and death. People who choose not to get older and more worrisome, like so many older people were, forever fearful about their upcoming last step.

Where would they be when it happened? That's what most worried about. No one wanted to be caught out accidentally dying on the street. Everyone wanted to die in the comfort of their home. With their loved ones. If you died on the street, the council workers were most uncouth when they came to carbonise you. You were treated like a piece of street garbage, such was the value of one's life. And they were quick to come. Having rotting corpses casually lying on the footpath wasn't a good look and was a community health hazard.

So, Forever27 is where some plan to die. Apparently, it's the best age to die. You are remembered in your prime. People come here to literally dance till they dropped. Attendees die in a rapture of music and lights, enjoying it down to the last second. Then...bang. They're expired. Just like that. No pain, no worries, just having a blast. The SLT devices automatically send a GPS signal to the cleaners as soon as the steps are empty. No one likes a corpse.

The nightclub had to close for a six-hour window every day to carbonise the remaining corpses and sweep them up, refresh the bar, and mop the floors. Some nights were busier than others. Sundays were the busiest. No one likes Mondays.

Elio arrives at the foreboding black double doors. The entrance to Forever27. The bouncers know him well, he is always here dancing away. They are suspicious of how someone can keep dancing with the ferocity and regularity that he does. They don't often see the same person more than once, most come here once and never leave. Occasionally there are regulars, but they are here to use up some steps before they turn 27. It's a timing thing. It hasn't been open long so there is no line yet, but people are steadily trickling in. This was the only time and space you could witness groups of people walking normally together. No funny gaits, no skates, no rolling, no striding, no stilting, no balling, no pogos.

They had no need for such antics, after all, they were coming here to dance and die.

Elio enters with a confident swagger. There is something about knowing he won't die as others drop around him that brings this confidence to a peak when he comes here. He feels invincible, and in comparison, he is. Elio is also hoping to see a girl he has had his eye on. He was surprised to see her at Forever27 three times already in the past two weeks.

He'd noticed her dancing, wild and tribal. Liberated and free-spirited. She just had this life in her he had not seen in anyone else. Elio was drawn to that energy. Something magnetic. Wow, could she dance. Hopefully she'll be here again tonight. If she is, he is planning to approach her and ask her out, he can't let her slip through one more time. This might be the last time he sees her if she's not already dead by now. Had she noticed him? He was pretty good at ripping up the dancefloor. Maybe she had seen him and was also curious about his continual return to the club without expiring.

Bass vibrations time perfectly with the strobing lights. Lasers cut through the thick haze, slicing it up like smoke sushi. It's dark. It's loud. The bar is open and so is the dancefloor. Let the games begin.

Elio looks around, scanning the room. As he surveys the bar area his eyes land on someone. Not because they want to naturally, but because he feels eyes on him and turns his head.

'Oh my god, she's here,' he says to himself. Eyes lock onto each other. She holds her drink up in cheers. He waves in return, then quickly drops his arm.

Because it's not who he is looking for. But the woman starts to stagger towards him, sloshing her drink from her cup all over the floor. It's hard to really see detail in the dark and smoke, but as she approaches it becomes clearer Elio is in trouble. She's not in good shape. She drapes her arm over him and attempts to give him a wink but both her eyes close and squint instead. She is shitfaced. Her eyes are all over the shop, rolling about in her cavern-like head. Her makeup looks as though it's been applied with a garden rake, and she clearly got her hair styling tips from a Maine Coon cat. She puts her wet lips up to his ear and whisper-mumbles something, licking his face as she pulls hers away.

That's the other thing about Forever27. It's a massive pickup place. Most people have been hesitant to waste their steps on sex their whole life so when they come here to die, they go the whole hog. Everyone is very direct, there's no need to waste time with getting-to-know-you protocol and niceties. There is no time to waste.

But she is not for him. He reels backwards out of her immediate reach radius, almost tripping over.

'Not happening, loony tunes,' Elio tells her. Just as blunt as her approach, he makes it known he's not interested. There's hunger in her eyes, she lunges again but he gracefully leaps and spins himself right out of harm's way, allowing her to fall to the floor like a water balloon, sprawling.

Thank you, Irish dancing skills. He heads towards the dance floor.

Everybody is having a blast. Really dancing. They are genuinely happy. They are free. It's invigorating. Then he sees it.

A man wearing a chequered mumu and dreadlocks goes down, crashing to the floor, taking out a bystander on his way. His SLT is flashing a red 'EXPIRED' on the screen.

A couple of minutes later, two cleaners arrive to carbonise him. One holding the carbonising rod, the other a long-handled metal dustpan and brush. The carbonising rod looks similar to a cattle prod. They just give you a 10-second poke and *zzzzztt zzzzzztttt*, you're fried so hot there is only a dry puddle of ash to be swept up and taken away. Pop it on your rose bushes. When you really think about it, it does seem a little brutal and uncaring, but no one even looks anymore. It's so commonplace. Especially here at Forever27.

Anyway, it's lucky he did die because the movement of his body from upright to the floor reveals behind him what Elio has been looking for.

Laser beams roving over her body, accentuating her form. That dance. Such carelessness and freedom behind it. She is lost in the music, dancing alone again. She doesn't see him yet. She doesn't see anyone. She is in her world and much to his delight, she is still alive. He starts his approach.

Chapter 7
THE PARTY

'Hello?' A greeting in a questioning tone. *Knock knock* on the door. Derek turns towards it.

'Come on in.' He uses the friendliest tone he can muster, it's high and light. Two heads pop around the door. Agnes and Aksel have found him.

It's the same reaction he always gets. The initial friendly surprise that everyone has. Then the look of disgust that flashes across their faces as the scene and smell hit them. Followed by fake niceties as they adjust to what they see before them. The tall one is twitching his nose, clearly unaccustomed to the steamed dim sim stench that Derek has become used to. It's been sitting down showers for him for a while now. Combine that with poor toilet hygiene and it's quite challenging in there. Derek always leaves his window open for this reason. No matter how cold or rainy it may be.

'Come in, come in. Can I fix you a drink?' Derek picks a couple of plastic cups out of the clutter on the table and empties a dead fly and a pair of dice out of one.

Frozen in the doorway after the initial shock, Agnes and Aksel cannot quite make out their host's features as he is silhouetted by the bright light streaming in the window behind him. But they do know he is a big, stinky man sitting down.

The room is dusty and musty, complete with lots of random things lying about haphazardly. Not too much on the floor though, there is a clear path big enough for his wheelchair to navigate the room. Just things upon things upon tables, chairs, sideboards, the fridge. Not much of a party vibe going on here, more rubbish tip vibes. They both notice an elaborate computer set up in the corner. It looks state-of-the-art and expensive. All types of coloured lights emerge from it, some blinking, some unblinking. You can hear the faint whirl of the cooling fans working overtime to sustain the beast. Screen was off but something was going on, it was busy flashing and humming away.

Agnes and Aksel look to each other, their eyes asking the same question without any words. It is not lost on Derek that aside from their heads looking in, they still have not moved past the doorway. He's going to have to start sweet-talking fast. Agnes decides she wants out. Looking at Aksel she now tries to evade going inside.

'Oh, sorry. I think we are at the wrong address. We'll leave you be.' They start to close the door and get the hell out of dodge when Derek changes tact.

'No, please. Wait.' There's a tinge of desperation in his voice. He's looking for their pity.

'I'm sorry. I really am. I...I just. I just wanted some company. I'm so lonely here.' He gestures to the wheelchair and manages to make his eyes water a little. 'I can't get down the stairs to meet anyone.' A genuine feeling and look of sadness comes over him. This part is true.

Agnes and Aksel look at each other. Having just formed their own fast friendship they both understand the difference it can make to one's well-being. And this man seems so lonely, stuck up here with no one to talk to but his supercomputer. No wonder he has invested so much into it, it's probably his only friend. Their heartstrings have been successfully pulled by Derek, of all people.

'My name's Derek.' His demeanour chirps up again, trying desperately to be inviting. His pity tactic seems to be working.

'Ahh. OK. We will come in for one drink.' Aksel caves in, quickly backing it up with, 'But we can't stay long, we are only passing by.'

'I understand. No doubt you are on your way to the lottery tonight. Lucky you. I would love to go, but...' Derek looks down at his chair. 'Please, come in and sit for 15 minutes. I'd just love to talk to another human for a while.' He nods towards the supercomputer, 'Esme is a good talker, but real people are better.' He forces a greasy smile of welcome, displaying his plaque-riddled teeth.

Agnes and Aksel finally bring their bodies to where their faces are, inside the door.

'Close the door, please.' Derek is quick to give instruction.

Aksel, aware of the stink, tries. 'It's a hot day. Would you mind if I let the breeze...'

'Close it!' Derek is snappy but now softens. 'Sorry, I struggle with agoraphobia.' He is impressed with his own pity party. Aksel closes the door.

Alone inside now, the three of them are awkward. Agnes breaks the ice.

'I'm Agnes and this is Aksel. Thanks for the invitation. Sure was a surprising way to receive it.'

'Oh, sorry if the plane hit you. It's the best way for me to talk to people outside. I've been communicating that way for years now.' Derek is trying his best to be engaging.

Aksel adds to the conversation, tries to lift it somewhat. 'They are well designed; they fly like a concord. I had a look at the way it was folded. Brilliant.' He's talking it up. Trying to relax everyone.

'I used to be an engineer, still kind of am. More on Esme now than practical hands-on stuff.' Derek's secretly a little bit chuffed. That's the nicest thing he can remember saying to him for a long, long time.

Uh oh...inner conflict stirs inside him. No, he decides to stay with the plan. He's not looking for friends, he's looking to harvest steps for his fitness regime.

Derek grabs the cups and starts to fill them with some clear liquid from an unlabelled, pre-used bottle smudged with grubby hand marks. Aksel watches on as he pours only two drinks.

'You're not having one with us? I thought this was a party,' Aksel asks curiously. Derek covers.

'Nah, I can't drink. It makes my diabetes loco. I save the good stuff for guests. I'll stick with water.' He gestures to his almost full cup. Hands the other two cups over to Agnes and Aksel.

'Cheers, happy lottery day. Good luck tonight, both of you.' Derek raises his cup to encourage them to drink up.

Agnes and Aksel raise theirs in unison. 'Cheers, and good luck.' Derek wolfs his down like a shot of tequila even though it's only water, trying to encourage them to follow suit. They look to each other questioningly.

'What is this anyway? There's no label on the bottle.' Aksel is becoming suspicious.

'If you have to ask, you're probably not ready for it.' Derek covers with a casual laugh. 'Just some home hooch which my brother made.' Derek smiles his lying face at them again. It's not hooch and he doesn't have a brother. It's a very strong dose of liquid temazepam. It should put them into a sleep orbit so deep they will become completely incapable of stopping Derek as he uses their nap time to harvest their steps. Last time he went a little too hard with the dose; his victim never woke after harvesting.

Oh well. Collateral damage. But he likes these two, he wants them to wake up. Hell, he even genuinely wants them to win the lottery tonight.

'Bottoms up, eh? I'll give you a refill,' Derek encourages. Agnes puts the cup to her lips as she steps towards the only source of freshness, the window. Her jacket catches on the corner of the table and jolts her back, spilling her drink everywhere.

'Careful! You silly girl! You're spilling it everywhere!' With a raised voice, Derek is frustrated and trying to rein it in. It's not easy for him to get his hands on the temazepam and he's annoyed at the wastefulness. He does not have much left, only what's left in the bottle.

Agnes and Aksel are both startled by Derek's quick change in demeanour, raised voice, and name-calling. They are now both alert, wary.

'Woah, calm down, it's only a drink,' Aksel interjects. 'No need to yell at her.' He looks to Agnes. Her face is shocked, confused, and unsure. She no longer wants to be here, that much is clear. She looks like she might cry.

'Maybe we might go, you don't really seem like you're up for guests. I feel like we are intruding.' Aksel is looking out for Agnes.

Desperate now, Derek apologises. 'Sorry, I...I didn't mean to. I don't get a lot of guests. My social skills need a bit of work.' He looks to his feet, 'Please stay and finish your drinks.' He's already pouring Agnes another.

Derek casually wheels his fat arse over in the wheelchair to land in front of the entrance door, effectively blocking them from exiting. All under the pretence of getting a book to show them. Aksel is still dubious. Derek's insistence that they drink the mysterious liquid, which he wants nothing to do with yet is fiercely protective over, does not sit well with him. It's now a firm no and he's ready to go. He makes the decision for them both.

'Actually, we need to keep moving. To be honest I don't really drink much. Shouldn't waste your brother's hooch though, would you like me to pour it back in the bottle?' Aksel asks Derek.

'Are you sure you don't want to try it? Please, it's pretty good. C'mon, my brother is looking for feedback. Please.' Derek is almost begging now, which spooks Agnes and Aksel even more.

'No. We're not drinking it. C'mon Agnes. We need to keep going,' says Aksel, now more firm.

'Her rolling can really slow us down, so we need extra time for travel.' Aksel directs this to Derek as he still blocks the doorway with his ample frame. He loathes to see this opportunity slip out of his grasp. Getting people up to his apartment isn't easy. He stares at them blankly, unmoving.

'Excuse us. It was nice to meet you, Derek, but we will be leaving now. Would you mind moving?' Aksel is insisting. The party is well and truly over.

'Please, I'll let you out once you have a drink, that's why you came here, isn't it? To party?' Derek doubles down. He's come this far and won't yield easily. But Aksel is becoming very short with Derek, he's starting to feel like they are being held hostage.

'We are going. We are not drinking your hooch. You need to move now before I move you myself.' Aksel is very direct now, all pleasantries gone, his tone serious. Agnes is like a deer caught in headlights, anxiously watching the battle of wills unfold.

The two men eyeball each other for a moment. No one moves. No one talks. They both know it's game over.

Aksel moves first. Quickly swinging his arm up and over his head, reaching behind into the top of his backpack, he grabs the big purple vibrator like he is taking a sword from its sheath. Holding it by the knob end, he swings it hard like a baseball bat, right into Derek's living donut face, the balls end connecting hard with his nose. A wet rainbow of crimson splatter explodes like a firecracker, giving the nearby walls a lovely smatter of colour. Derek's head lolls about like a buoy on a troubled ocean, blood gushing from his nose, down his face, down his 14 chins, and pools on one of the 23 fat rolls he borrowed from the Michelin Man. He's out. But for how long no one knows.

'Agnes, quick. Give me your drink. Let's give him a taste of his own medicine.' Aksel looks to Agnes, who was completely unprepared for the giant purple vibrator attack. She's stunned, standing there mute. She's unfamiliar with violence and her eyes are big, looking at the blood gushing out, not really hearing Aksel. 'Agnes! Quickly!'

She snaps to, grabs the drink, and passes it to Aksel.

'Now you drink, motherfucker.' Aksel is talking more to himself than Derek. He grabs Derek's hair, yoinks his head back, and pours the liquid down his throat. He's curious to stick around and see what will happen to him but he wants out of this stinking, greasy hellhole right now.

It takes both Agnes and Aksel to move Derek and his wheelchair out of the doorway, a trail of blood dripping the way. His body all floppy. Head down. Aksel puts the vibrator in Derek's arms, the tip of it in his mouth.

'No, I insist. You keep it, Derek.' He turns it on, has a little giggle to himself.

He finds himself checking his SLT for the second time today. It's very unlike him to do so, breaking his own rule. The craziness of the morning and unexpected 'party' has put him on edge.

'Let's go, Agnes.'

Chapter 8
SARITA

17 YEARS, 168CM, 62KG. FREEFALLER AKA LIVING BLIND.

Lost in herself, the lights, and the music, Sarita does not notice the dying chequered mumu man being carbonised or Elio's approach. 17 years young. Won't live past 22 at this rate but who's counting? Not Sarita, that's for sure.

Sarita is constantly pushing life's boundaries. Even though she would describe herself as a loner, she loves experiencing everything possible, where possible. Hiking, paragliding, bicycling, wrestling, dancing. Oh, she loves to dance. Put on some dirty bass and nothing can hold her down. And sex. Sarita is one of the few people who continues to have sex. She is not worried about tripping her SLT because she has never had one. And never will.

Growing up in a commune taught her a few things about freedom that the rest of society will never have the opportunity to understand. She is living blind. And it probably won't be for much longer but fuck a duck, she is having a ball.

Being born in a commune, she was not privy to what others had known as normal.

Being born in a commune, she did not know about SLTs.

She never had the option.

Being born in a commune, she didn't even know who her parents were.

Being born in a commune, everybody treated everybody as their own.

It was better this way, given everyone who lived there died young. They didn't know why. And people were dying every month. More than one, usually two to six people depending on what was happening at the commune. The death toll was always higher on doof nights. To be expected, I suppose. All that dancing.

Sure, it's a high death rate, but the high sex rate in the commune offsets this, with two to four babies being added to the group every month.

Originally the commune was born out of dissidents who refused to participate in the SLT regime and get one fitted when it was introduced. They thought they were safe, and still did to this day. Unbeknown to them, their DNA was already changed before they fled for the hills to start their 'freedom camp'. Control started happening way before that. Opposition was expected and the government was one step ahead. Secretly and quietly, it had started its work through populous immunisation programs and nanobots in drinking water. You were in it even if you didn't know it or want it. You were on a timer with or without an SLT. You had no rights as the move was deemed essential for humankind's survival.

The commune population usually stood somewhere between 16 000 to 19 000 people, give or take.

It was enough to sustain their own self-sufficient farming practices, water management, and infrastructure. Infrastructure mostly being communal housing for the population. There were a few community halls and group sports grounds but no hospitals, schools, or other governmental-type places. There was no governing body. If you were sick, the community looked after you. However, due to the importance of keeping the birth rate going, they did have birthing units where the most 'qualified' women worked to help ensure the children survived. They were less worried about the mother the more children she'd already birthed.

Sometimes people left to find more in life, not entirely believing all their bullshit. Fed up with working the fields every day. Everyone had a job to do to contribute to the group. Some people just wanted more adventure, wanted to know more about the world, so they left too. Some women didn't want to be incubators and would rather take their chances in the wild. But 90% of the population accepted and did their duties without question.

Reproduction is essential for their survival. If the rate of reproduction fell even to just one baby a month, there would be devastating consequences for the commune. It would become unsustainable within the decade. So, sex has become an essential part of their survival and freedom.

Sustainability of the commune was firmly placed on the women. Every woman was expected to have at least three to six births. Births, not children, because they were more of a commodity to keep the commune going than a personal being to nurture.

Fuck that. Sarita was having none of it. She liberated herself at the ripe old age of 14, not long after she got her first period. That's when the expectations of getting pregnant start. That's when the men start sniffing around, trying to 'help' with her obligation. She was just a child herself and had zero interest in producing one. So one night, while the doof was on and everyone was busy dancing and dying, she left with nothing but a handful of unshelled, unsalted peanuts, some green vegetables from the communal garden, a bottle of water, and a lust for life.

She didn't choose to be living blind, she never had that option. Sarita is a freefaller.

*

Spinning wildly, pixie-like face to the lights as though they're the first ray of sunshine after a dreary winter, Sarita is living her best life. The dirty bass she loves throbbing through her body, vibrating her core. Skin glistening with sweat and lights, she looks like a human mirror ball.

As Elio gets closer, he can also see her lips moving, singing something to herself.

He starts dancing and he is out to impress. Dancing his way closer to her through the smoke and lasers. It's not the best music for Irish dancing but the beat is fast, pacing his feet. *Bump. Bump.*

He purposefully accidentally dances into Sarita.

Her spinning stops but she's still dancing as she turns to find an interesting face mouthing the word 'sorry' through the loud music. She is intrigued by him. The first thing she notices is his dancing, the furiously fast legs. But more importantly, how he was dancing, Irish style. It is not something you see a lot, for sure. Then she notices his face. Smooth shaven. Dimples. Quite good looking. Young.

Exuding a zest for life, not in the least like they have come here to die tonight, as others have.

Sarita is starting to like what she sees and is curious about him. She starts dancing with the surprise man and he dances back at her. It's like watching an exotic bird mating ritual. Pop up and down here, spin there. If Elio had feathers, they would definitely be fanned out. The couple puts in a good 25 minutes' dance foreplay together before Sarita motions she needs a drink and offers Elio to follow. He obliges like a lost puppy, following her anywhere.

It's quieter at the bar and they introduce themselves and strike up a conversation. The sexual chemistry between them is undeniable. They are drawn to each other, an instant bond. Gazing at one another. The bartender hands them their drinks. As Sarita grabs hers, Elio notices she is not wearing an SLT. Strange, maybe she is left-handed. He looks down at her other hand. Still no SLT.

Ankle maybe. His eyes wander downward. No. From what he can tell, this woman before him somehow does not have one. Maybe a black-market dealer like him had stolen it? Now she is even more intriguing. He must know.

'Would you like to go outside for a while, it's pretty stuffy in here.' Elio looks pointedly to a young lady being carbonised a few metres away. It can smell a bit BBQ-like in the first few seconds. Sarita follows his eye line to the carbonising.

'Great idea, I could do with some fresh air. And I'd like to get to know you more.' She leads the way out.

Chapter 9
THE JOURNEY

Agnes and Aksel gasp in a big lungful of fresh air. Aksel is coughing. They are back outside after eluding Derek in his stinky, waste-strewn apartment. Their adrenaline is pumping. It's not often one finds themselves in a fight using a giant purple vibrator as a truncheon. Agnes is first to speak.

'What in the hell just happened in there? Some party. What do you suppose he was trying to make us drink?' She is puffing from the quick escape down the stairwell.

'I'm not even sure what was going on in there,' Aksel says, still unclear on Derek's intention. Everything about the encounter leaves them baffled. The invitation, the mess, the stench, the 'party', the insistence on drinking. Derek himself and even his supercomputer are like bit part players in a B-grade movie.

'Is he…? Did you…? Is he dead?' Agnes is a little concerned. She isn't really the murdering type.

'Ahh. Not sure but probably not. The vibrator only knocked him out, he was still breathing. I guess that depends on whatever the drink was that I poured down his neck.'

His casualness about the situation doesn't sit well with Agnes. She shifts uncomfortably. Unsure how she feels about this, she diverts her eyes from Aksel's gaze, looking to the ground. She raises her hands and massages her forehead as though she has a headache as the weight of what just happened starts to hit home. She has never been involved in anything like this before. Aksel can see she is anxious. He tries to reassure her.

'Don't feel bad for him, his intention was not good. I only gave him what he was trying to get us to drink so consider it karma. Don't waste your time thinking about him anymore.' He's quick to brush over it and get on with the day. 'C'mon, let's get moving. It's not long till the lottery starts, we've got to get to the stadium.'

There are a lot of people about now, using their various modes of 'walking' to get to the stadium. It's chaotic and messy to watch, a type of visual pollution.

Other rollers, skaters, stilt walkers, gliders. The pole vault guy, Gregory, is vaulting away, covering good ground. Like Turquoise Fitzenberger, there are a few other wealthy people being carried about. One on a throne carried by four, another just being piggybacked on some poor sucker's back who was struggling in the heat of the day. Not rich enough to have four carriers but not poor enough for no carriers. This class of people didn't fit in with the everyday person. They were mocked by the wealthy for only having one carrier, and mocked by the average person for trying to be something they were not. Strangely, they were often without friends as they struggled to be someone meaningful in a place with no reason.

The never-ending entertaining parade of assorted 'walkers' push past a smitten Elio and Sarita as they slowly stroll through the streets, hand in hand. They have already wantonly had sex. They are both on a high. The build-up of finally meeting Sarita after lusting after her for so long has left Elio in a highly elated state. He's quite sure he's in love. But he's not sure what it means for her to have no SLT. She seems unfazed by it all. But he's curious and he must ask.

'So, I really like you. A lot.' Elio hesitates, decides to dive straight in. 'What's the deal with you not wearing a tracker? Did you ever have one? Did someone steal it?'

'What do you mean? What tracker?' Sarita looks confused.

Elio touches on his SLT. There is a hint of fun sarcasm in his voice.

'Gee, I don't know. Maybe it's these fuckers everyone is forced to wear.'

Sarita looks to his tracker. 'Oh, those things. The ball and chain you're all connected to. No thank you. Funny, I thought they were just watches. You know, for telling the time.'

Elio looks at her questioningly, 'Yeah, I guess they do tell the time in a way. The time you have till you die.' Sarita looks back at him, matter-of-fact.

'Well, I've never had one, that means I'm free. Lucky me!' She's excited. Bounces up and down. This girl has some pep for life. Elio stares in disbelief and gently stops her from bouncing, wasting her steps.

Sarita looks at him. 'I have learned about them from people I've met. I understand their purpose, they give you a limit to your step and lifespan, right?'

Now it's Elio's turn to be confused. 'I don't understand how you could never have got one. Everyone must get one when they are born. They are unremovable.'

'Well, I never have. There's something you should know about me.' She stops and takes a breath. 'I grew up in a commune. No one had these...things on their wrists.' She flicks Elio's SLT with disdain.

Sarita downloads her background to Elio, who is surprised by the culture of the commune. Surprised to know they even exist. This is new to him. It sounds fun, actually, if you brush over the abuse of girls and women as incubators for the children part. This explains a lot about Sarita's free spirit and not giving a damn. Her enjoyment and lust for life. These traits that drew him to her.

Then it dawns on him like a hot summer morning. So glaring. So undeniable.

She could die at any moment, maybe even after her next step. She's done a lot of dancing throughout her life. How long has she got left? Sarita can feel the downcast shift in him from elated, to suddenly worrisome as she watches his face drop.

'What's wrong?' She misreads his mood change. 'Don't you like me now? Because of the commune thing? Because if it is, I can...'

'No, that's not it. I like the commune thing. It suits you,' Elio cuts her off. Smiling at her, he wavers, decides to be blunt. The smile drops again.

'You probably don't know because of the commune but your body is still on a tracker, even if you did not get one of these attached at birth.' He touches his SLT. She looks at him questioningly, not quite understanding.

'What do you mean? Explain please.'

'I mean, SLT or not, our bodies have been genetically and biologically changed over the decades, before we even knew what was happening. We've been reprogrammed inside to what we used to be. This was happening long before SLTs were even thought of.' Sarita's face reads confusion. He continues.

'The government brought in the Step Longevity Trackers to give people more control and decision-making around how they would use their steps. It doesn't actually limit your steps; it just tells you how many more you have left.'

He can see Sarita is struggling with this new information. He keeps explaining.

'SLTs give everyone's life a bit more structure. No one has to wonder how far away they are from death anymore. The data is right there on your wrist.' He flicks his wrist up to show her the face of the SLT.

'Basically, it was their way to make people feel like they had control over their own lives again. You know, keep the masses calm lest they risk a mass uprising and possible mutiny.' It's said with jest and sarcasm but the two know there's some truth in it. They share a little nervous giggle, realising an uprising is not entirely off the agenda. The government should be concerned.

'Yeah, I didn't think about that. I suppose people would have been very angry when everything changed.' Sarita is getting it. 'Trick them into thinking they still have power. Brilliant scam.'

'So, I'm assuming you are also unaware you have only been allocated 60 000 000 steps for your lifespan, it's about 40 years,' Elio continues, 'then you die, or expire, as they like to call it. Every living cell in your body will cease to be.' He says the last sentence grandly as he swoops his arm in one swift motion, trailing the horizon. Sarita looks to him, he can see the penny is dropping for her. She's thinking.

'So, what you are saying is...I could...are you saying I too am destined to die from this, but because I don't have one of those watches, I won't know when?' Sarita's mind whirls with the reality of the situation she now finds herself in.

'It's an SLT. Step Longevity Tracker. And yes, that's what I'm saying. Every step you take shortens your lifespan. Even cycling, even sex. Any leg movement like a step will take from your lifespan. Have you not noticed all the crazies around us? People walking oddly? Look around.' He gestures to the ever-growing crowds around them.

'I just thought that's how it was out here.' Sarita's brain is on overload. 'Everyone in the commune walked normally, like me. We had no need for this behaviour.' She corrects herself. 'We did not know we had a need for this behaviour.'

'And you sound like you've done a lot of dancing in your life so far.' Elio is straight to the point. He's genuinely concerned for her now, his brows creasing, thinking about how he could help her.

No one speaks for a moment. They are both still on the

street. Facing each other, holding hands. White noise and craziness around them.

Elio has made his decision.

Aksel is whistling the tune 'Rollin', having some fun with Agnes as she rolls beside him. He's also doing the air arse spank motion, waving his arm around in front of him. His knees bending and straightening, bobbing him up and down. With his height, it's quite comical to see. All limbs, air spanking some arse. Head popping up and down, gangster style. The only thing missing is a bandana wrapped around his head.

'Stop now!' She's giggling. 'You're supposed to be helping me, not taunting me.' He can't help laughing either. Any time he has to look at Agnes with her swimming goggles on it always gives him a giggle.

A genuine friendship has struck up between them. A big brother/little sister type of relationship. The narrow escape from Derek only strengthened the bond of their fast friendship. They are completely at ease with one another now.

'Wanna go back and get some more vibrators? Derek's using mine,' Aksel jokes.

'No!' She's got the cackles up. 'Enough vibrators for today.'

'Well, we need another weapon, what if we get in another fight?' He's poking, having fun.

'I doubt anything else like that could possibly happen to us today. That was crazy.' She's still absorbing the scenario earlier at Derek's.

'Let's keep moving, the stadium gates will be opening soon.' Agnes is aware that her rolling will slow them down. They set off towards the centre of the city, where the stadium is located.

The loudhailer noise of Turquoise catches on the breeze every now and then, providing a distorted background noise for their journey. It's a lovely afternoon.

*

'Let's go Sarita. Get on my back. We can't risk you taking one more step. After all the dancing you've done in the commune growing up. You never know how close you are.' This is fun for her. She climbs on, wrapping Elio in a warm embrace, locking on like a claw hair clip. He starts walking.

'But what about you?' She is curious and confused. 'How come you can walk normally? You don't seem worried at all about your steps. And what about all the people at the club? They walk normally and dance and they don't care about steps either.' She is carpet-bombing him with questions, trying to wrap her head around everything. Elio attempts to explain.

'OK, slow down. Forever27 is a suicide hotspot. People choose to go there to die. They want to spend their last steps enjoying themselves. Dancing and having sex. They don't care because they are there to die.'

'I guess that's why I could never pick up.' Her response is light, with a wry smile. 'Aside from Forever27 of course, it was so easy there. I picked you up quickly.'

Elio continues, glazing over her attempt at lightening the tone.

'If you've ever stayed the whole night, you will notice 97% of the patrons die. Remember how the girl was being carbonised when we were talking at the bar?'

'Well, yes, but again, I just thought that was what always happened out here. We used to bury our dead.' Sarita is blissfully ignorant in the ways of the outside world.

'Out here, we carbonise,' Elio explains. 'Too many people to bury. Burial is a very old-fashioned, time-consuming thing to do. Carbonisation is quick, easy, and sanitary. We cannot have bodies lying on the streets and inside establishments where they drop. It's a public health hazard.'

Turquoise Fitzenberger and her throne-carrying slaves approach them on her last round before the lottery starts.

She's still screaming through the loudhailer in everyone's faces as they pass her, reminding them about tonight's lottery. She really wants everyone to go.

Sarita is fascinated by her; she can't tear her eyes away as Turquoise gets closer.

'Who is that? And why is she on a throne? What's with the yelling at everyone through the loudhailer?' Sarita needs answers. Now she knows everything is not at all how she thought it was.

'That's Turk-kwoise.' He pronounces her name the same way Turquoise says it. 'She's the mayor of Sunshine City. Turk-kwoise Fitzenberger. She's wealthy, so she buys people to carry her around so she won't have to waste her own steps. It's a class thing.'

'A what thing? What's a class?' She'd never heard of such a thing before. Everyone in the commune had always been treated equally.

Turquoise, now face to face with them, raises the loudhailer and yells, 'Don't forget the lottery tonight! Gates open in one hour!' She is very generous with her saliva as she talks, spraying those close by in a viscous shower. Turquoise and her slaves trudge away, still yelling. But not before Elio pickpockets her. Karma.

'Sheez. She is a lot. Who even voted for her.' Elio is overwhelmed by her mere presence and air of superiority. He watches her with distaste as she is carried away.

'Class is about money and power,' he explains, 'the more money and power you have, the more of an arsehole you can be without any recourse. Turk-kwoise is very wealthy. She bought her slaves to carry her around and do things for her so she wouldn't have to use steps. It's pathetic really.' He hated this type of person. Yes, he was a step thief himself, but he was an ethical one. He never made others feel lesser or downtrodden. Never thought he was above anyone.

'Huh,' was all Sarita could muster. She couldn't believe this crap!

She gazes across the crowds, taking in the oddities that surround her. It is good people-watching. She spots one of the more interesting-looking people approaching whom she has seen around quite a bit. He is very distinct-looking. Large man in stature, wears yellow, always has a rolling sack. She is so curious about him.

'What about that guy? What's his story? I see him around a lot.' She has become a knowledge sponge, wanting to soak up everything.

'To be honest, I don't know much about him. I've seen him about but we've never talked. He's not a part of any of my circles.' Elio shifts his weight. His legs are starting to become restless again. 'I got to keep moving.'

Aksel and Agnes shuffle their way through the crowd, away from Derek's douche den towards the stadium. They pass a seemingly carefree, cute young couple, him kindly carrying his girlfriend on his back. The couple is lost in discussion and clearly oblivious to everything and everyone around them. It's not very often you see couples around like this. Agnes studies them as she passes. She wonders how two people can come together in such unreasonable circumstances and behave like there is nothing wrong in the world. They seem so at peace. Except for his legs, she notes they can't seem to stay still. Agnes admires them with a tinge of jealousy. It's all she ever wanted. To be someone's someone. So simple, yet so hard to attain. Always out of reach. Being a roller was not exactly an attractive trait to others, even more so in a world where dating and sex were not really a thing anymore. She accepted that she would probably be single her whole life.

Agnes looks to Aksel. She likes him, but not in that way. He is attractive, but she is not attracted to him. She sees him as more of a protector. Agnes reminds herself that this easy friendship with him is also a great relationship to be in. Also, she was concerned when he chose the biggest, most offensive coloured vibrator out of the sex toy swamp.

Ahead, Big John Sweeney crosses before them. He is easy to spot, he only dresses in yellow. As always, he is lugging his sack of mysterious items behind him. He was never seen without his sack. No one knew what was in that sack, but the shape would change almost daily. It was a heavy, navy-coloured canvas sack, worn but without holes.

The sack lived on a skateboard, dragging behind him. A piece of rope tightly tied around the top led up to Big John's massive bicep. There it coiled around the upper part, tied off in a bow. According to Big John, it's important to use a bow instead of a knot just in case you have to release it quickly. He'd learned that lesson from the other arm, now limp and useless, dangling at his side.

Which explained another reason why he had a huge bicep, it was the only bicep doing all the work. It looked like a Popeye arm!

'Hey, Big John. How are you going, man?' enquires Aksel. His manner was casual, calm, and friendly. Aksel knows Big John could flip the switch at any moment. He's seen him lose his shit with others before and vowed to never be on that end of John. Other than that, he was a fairly friendly guy. He didn't hang out with John like friends do, they were more 'business acquaintances'. John didn't really have any friends in the true sense of the word. He was a bit of a loner, always got about on his own, never seen enjoying the company of others. Even still, he had enough social skills to hold a conversation. They'd always been respectful towards one another. Although John did involve himself in petty crime, he was kind of decent. Big John had morals.

'Eh yeh, Ax. Y'know...yeh man just hustlin' just y'know, dude, yeh eh.' The English language wasn't Big John's strong suit. Nevertheless, Aksel always treated him with respect. And he has used Big John's services before, scoring a nice pair of designer runners. In fact, he is wearing them now, though they're a little worse for wear after going through the park with Agnes.

Big John notices. 'Yeh, sweet kicks innit yeh, Ax, eh?'

'Yes, my friend. Thank you.' He gives John a little courtesy bow. 'I'll catch up with you later.' Aksel is keen to keep moving. Agnes definitely wants to keep moving. She's at ground level in rolling position and his skateboard sack load seems to be trying to pick a fight with her for ground area. Constantly bumping against her.

She pipes up. 'Yes, lovely to meet you, let's go, Aksel.'

'Eeh yer tonight in oval, yeh. Dunno go. Dunno go.' Big John's expression turns serious. 'Dunno go, Ax.' At that, he checks his SLT, turns on his heels, and leaves. The skateboard jerkily spins around to catch up with him, the end of it catching Agnes in the face. What should have been a black eye is not. But her swimming goggles are now cracked through one eyepiece.

'Well, he was adorable. A friend of yours, huh?' She allows a small giggle. 'What language does he speak?' she asks Aksel.

'He's somewhat more of an acquaintance. He speaks Sweeney.' He gives her a playful kick-start and she starts rolling. 'Keep moving, sister.'

'Sir! Yes, sir.' She mocks his order, saluting.

As they set off again, there is a new noise coming their way. *Fwop...fwop...fwop.* It sounds 'bouncy' but littered with cries for help...

'So, what about you? Tell me why you don't seem to be worried about your steps? You've been at the club dancing a lot. I've noticed you don't even care about looking at your tracker watch thingo.'

Sarita's still on Elio's back as they push through the ever-increasing crowds, leaning her head down to speak into his ear.

'Why? What's going on with you?' She is still slightly overwhelmed by all she has learned today.

'All will be revealed very soon, Sarita, we are nearly there.' Elio is calm and measured.

'Why are we going in the opposite direction to everyone else?' Sarita finally notices. 'Shouldn't we be going to the lottery too? I'm going to die soon. Where are you taking me?' She is starting to get anxious.

'We're not far now, we're going to a place where I can help you,' Elio placates. 'But you must never talk about what happens there to anyone, ever. OK?' Sarita looks confused and concerned. 'OK, Sarita? Trust me. Please.' Elio pushes the point. A firm look into Sarita's eyes tells her he is very serious.

'OK, Elio, OK I get it.' She has resigned herself to trusting him completely.

They finally arrive at the bottom of a dingy flight of stairs to Derek's apartment and Elio drops Sarita to the ground. A rancid smell is lingering, seeping from the entrance. It's dark and questionable. Sarita stops dead in her tracks. She is now starting to wonder if Elio has set her up for something more sinister than he is making out. Really, she doesn't actually know him at all and starts to question her naivety and willingness to follow a stranger. She didn't know about all the stuff Elio was telling her about today, and she just believed him. It did explain a lot of things though.

She decides she has come this far, and she is going to die anyway, so fuck it. And she likes him. Overall, she is satisfied his intentions are good, so she commits fully, takes a deep, long breath of fresh air, and follows Elio into the stairwell, holding onto the back of his t-shirt for good measure.

'Why are we going in here? I don't like it.' For some reason she feels a need to whisper close to Elio's ear. He likes it.

'Shh...wait. I'll explain when we get there.' They proceed up the stairs as quietly as possible, arriving at a door where the smell seems to be coming from. Na-ah. Sarita motions a 'no' with her head, but Elio ignores her and turns the doorknob.

Fwop...fwop...fwop. More cries for help, screaming, getting closer. Aksel and Agnes are both curious and concerned, trying to see what's coming their way.

'What in the hell is that? It is coming closer.' Agnes can't see yet because she is on the ground but Aksel, the human fire watch tower, can see the sun bouncing off something that's also bouncing.

The fucking ballers.

He hated the ballers, they seemed to cause trouble and chaos every time, everywhere they went. He should have guessed earlier, the cries for help and screaming were dead giveaways there were ballers or punks close by.

'Little fuckwits.' Aksel can't hide his contempt.

'What? What is it Aksel? I can't see.' Agnes rubs her goggles, which does nothing to help.

'It's those idiot ballers. Seven of them. Got a mind to spike them on their way past. Burst their bubbles.' Aksel really does not like them at all.

Agnes stands and removes her goggles to see.

'Oh, those dickheads knocked my friend into the river, she got washed down to the sewerage waste area. It was not pretty.'

Here they come, bouncing downhill, out of control, taking out random people here and there. Bouncing inside their big clear, sweaty plastic balls. One goes straight into a stilt-walker and sends him toppling over like bowling pins, eating the cement footpath with his head and shoulders. Blood explodes from his head as he starts to wail in pain. One of his legs is bent at an unnatural angle. The ballers don't care. They can't just stop easily. They just keep on balling.

That's one major drawback to choosing to be a baller. You

can't just stop. Coming down the hill they are unstoppable and unsteerable, kind of like running with bulls. Just as dangerous.

Sure, there was the potential to cover large amounts of ground if you did it right, but there were just too many things that could go wrong, and they were too unpredictable. Not only did ballers injure and sometimes even kill other people, they also quite often injured themselves, sometimes resulting in their own death. One was found dead in their ball floating seven kilometres off the coast just last month. It wasn't good. After floating around in their plastic, clear coffin with the sun beating down on them relentlessly for weeks, they were slowly poached. Sous vide, I think they call it. They had to pour the liquidised body out! Aksel didn't think it was a wise choice as a mode of transport, which made sense because only the idiots and riff-raff seemed to pick balling as their way to get around.

Erring on the side of caution, Agnes and Aksel both put themselves out of harm's way, cowering behind an electrical transformer box on the street. *Fwop...fwop...fwop...fwop. Fwop... fwop...fwop.*

'Incoming idiots! Brace yourself!' Aksel gives Agnes a heads-up. The first three *fwop* on by without incident. The fourth and fifth are going in the right direction, clear of innocent bystanders, but the two people inside have lost control. They have lost their footing and are being thrown around wildly inside, like a human washing machine. They are squealing. It looks like it has been going on for a while, they barely have any fight left in them, just letting the ball toss them like ragdolls.

The sixth one, the one who hit the stiltwalker earlier, seems to know what he's doing. He has full control of the ball. It makes one wonder if he hit the stiltwalker for sport. Probably.

Finally, the last ball is bouncing down, out of control, ricocheting off trees, street furniture, and light poles. Like a pinball game. The figure inside is being thrown about quite violently. It hits the rubbish bin and bounces off straight towards them at speed.

Fwop. Straight onto the transformer they are using as a shield. It hits the top, the ball overhangs as the downward pressure turns it oval-shaped upon contact. The person inside also connects with the bottom, with force, pushing their face hard up against the inside of the plastic person hole, distorting it. Making them look like a squishy, sweaty specimen squeezed in a jar. This is what Aksel and Agnes are greeted with when they look up. A split second of absolute terror in the baller's eyes. Then physics takes control again and the ball unsquashes and just as quickly leaps back into the air to continue its treacherous journey, the victim trapped firmly inside.

Agnes and Aksel pop their heads back up from behind the transformer. That was a close one.

'I'm confident the balls are actually eating the people inside.' Aksel is bemused.

'Seems like they deserve to be eaten.' Agnes has an adrenaline giggle.

If Sarita thought the stairwell stank, that was just the entrée. As soon as Elio opens the apartment door the smallest crack, the stench envelops her completely. If it were a cartoon, there would definitely be those wavy, green-coloured stink lines coming from it. She gags a little.

'What...no...we're going in there? Voluntarily?' She looks at Elio, uncomfortable. 'Seriously? You're serious?' She's hoping he's playing a trick on her.

'Yes, Sarita. It's a small price to pay for your freedom. Don't be scared, I know him. He won't hurt us.' Elio tries to comfort and put her at ease.

'Well, I forgot to bring my hazmat suit, so...' Sarita really doesn't want to enter.

'We won't be long,' Elio cuts her off. 'The longer you stand here, the longer we breathe shit vapour. Your choice.'

Sarita now takes the lead, puts on her big girl pants, swings the door open, and enters first.

The window is open, a gentle breeze caresses the curtain lazily. A juxtaposition to the rest of the room, it is still dark and stinky inside. It takes a few seconds for their eyes to adjust. It is also quiet. Too quiet. No one has greeted them, but the door is unlocked. Elio knows Derek always likes the door locked, that's why he enjoys sneaking up on him. It's a game, to show him locked doors did not equal privacy or safety.

Elio scans the familiar surroundings; he notices some nice fresh red splatters across the wall before his eyes fall to the blood trail on the floor. His eyes follow the blood trail to find the source. It's Derek.

He's hunched over in his chair, clutching something. His head is moving. It's hard to see from the door so Elio circles around to face Derek. Sarita hasn't even noticed Derek. She is slack-jawed and staring with wide eyes. Staring at nothing in particular, yet everything. The whole scene seems to put her into some sort of shock-induced trance. She hasn't moved or said a word since she entered but seems fixated on Derek's toilet bucket and wiping mop in the corner.

Elio can now see Derek has blood on his face. And he is clutching a giant purple vibrator, the tip of it in his mouth, propping up his head. The vibrator is on, his head floppily wiggling about like a bobblehead toy. He notices the smashed-in nose. Derek's wet, bubbling breathing alerts Elio to the fact he is not dead, but he is well and truly out.

'What sort of weird shit are you into, Derek, you sick fuck,' Elio says, talking more to himself than Sarita. This snaps Sarita out of her daze, she turns to look at Elio, noticing him with some other guy in a wheelchair who is fellating a giant purple vibrator. There is blood dripping down it. Elio is kneeling beside him, studying him intensely. Slapping his cheeks to try and wake him up.

'Woah. OK. This is...this is...who is this, Elio? I'm scared to ask, but what is going on?' She keeps looking towards the door, calculating how many steps it would take to get out of dodge.

'This is Derek,' Elio explains. 'He was going to help us restore your step quota. He works for me.' Derek's head is still bobbing for apples as the vibrator maintains a steady pace.

'Can you turn that off, please,' Sarita interjects. 'It's just too weird for me.' Elio turns it off, Derek's head stops dancing like some kind of macabre Halloween decoration. Everything is still. Esme, Derek's supercomputer, adds a few short beeps to the mood and the cooling fans whirl into action. This takes their attention off Derek for a while as they both turn to look at it. It's flashing and whirling, demanding attention. Elio updates Sarita.

'That is why we are here. Esme. That's the computer's name, according to Derek. I think it's the only girlfriend he's ever had.' He laughs at his own joke. 'It is purpose-built to harvest steps from people, then upload them into other people.' Sarita walks over to have a closer look, fascinated by all the gadgetry. There was nothing like this in the commune.

'That's why I bought you here and that's why I never worry about how many steps I am using. I was planning to upload you to maximum capacity. Like me,' Elio continues, 'but I may need Derek's help, he knows how to use the computer, he built it.' Elio looks over Esme methodically.

'I guess I can give it a go. I'm savvy, but I don't know...' As he walks towards the computer, he notices three men out the window crossing the street. They are walking in a normal fashion. No care taken to conserve steps. Dressed entirely in black. This sets his alarm bells off. They are walking with purpose, towards Derek's apartment, stepping in unison. Elio's heart sinks. He knows them.

'Wow. They think I attract attention. Look at these goons.

They couldn't be more obvious.' Elio is talking to himself but Sarita is listening. She gets a sense of wariness.

The men are from the blackwork gang he used to work for. That's how he met Derek. And they are keen to chop off Elio's feet to teach him a lesson for leaving, going solo, and supposedly showing off and attracting unwanted attention to the gang. If they find him in Derek's apartment he will not be leaving in one piece.

'Shit!' Elio quickly ducks down. 'Get down, quickly,' he instructs Sarita. She complies.

It's been an interesting, fun, and slightly dangerous trip into the stadium for Agnes and Aksel. They are in good spirits and relatively unscathed from the journey. There is an easiness with each other and they both care about each other's well-being and safety.

It is not long now till the lottery starts and everyone is waiting for the gates to open. The surrounding area is now heaving with the chaos of various movements. A visual cacophony. People are starting to get excited, a loud buzz of conversation overlays everything.

The whole situation is a sensory overload. Five people circle overhead in their homemade gyrocopters, trying to scare the ones in their homemade gliders. They've long been rivals in the sky, the gyro boys claiming the gliders have Icarus syndrome. The gliders could not care any less about the gyro boys, they are sick of being buzzed by them, they are bullies. The ballers are already here, some of them in blood-splattered balls, taking up more than their fair share of room in their radius of plastic. The stiltwalkers, towering over everyone, peeking over the fence into the stadium. The rollers, covered in muck. The skaters, complete with bleeding knees and elbows. Gregory and friends have successfully made it with their pole vaults and, of course, there are the carriers, the lowest class. They are burdened by the weight of their rich owners, metaphorically and physically.

The screeching and trumpet playing starts to come into earshot as Turquoise Fitzenberger appears at the gate. She, of course, is getting carried on her throne by her four people. She has the loudspeaker on loud.

'Welcome, everybody to the annual Sunshine City Lottery.' Half words, half spittle. 'I now declare the lottery festival open.' Two workers come in from each side to open the gate. Aksel could swear one was Big John Sweeney, but he is not close enough to be sure. He finds it odd, Big John never comes to community events. He always just does his own thing. He refuses to live in hope like everyone else does.

Just as the gates finish opening, one of Fitzenberger's carriers uses his last step and goes down hard. He dramatically falls lifeless to the ground in front of everybody, causing his corner of the throne to hit the deck. This catches Turquoise off guard and she topples to the ground, clutching her loudhailer, landing on her face and shoulders upside down. A collective *'ooh!'* ripples through the waiting crowd. Ungracefully, her dress flops over her head, exposing her Strawberry-themed adult nappy underwear and control tights. The collective *'ooh!'* now turns to a collective *'agh!'* as Turquoise gives away her secret. She is so embarrassed at this undignified situation that she is happy her face is covered by her skirt, so no one can see how red it is.

Before the carbonisers can even get to the fallen carrier for carbonisation, the crowd starts to pour in, squeezing through the bottleneck of the gate. No one cares to help Turquoise as they rush past for the best spots, stampeding over the dead carrier.

'Fuck you, Turk-kwoise!' says one of the skaters, giving her a nappy wedgie as they skate past. A couple of people may have 'accidentally' stood/rolled on her on their way in, such was her popularity with the public. Someone snatched her loudhailer and yelled, 'Turk-kwoise, you elitist maggot!' in a mocking manner, straight into her ear. How the tide has turned on Turquoise Fitzenberger. The disrespect! All she can do now is brace herself until the hoards have entered the stadium and hope nothing gets broken. Most people chose to suck up to the mayor, it could be beneficial for them. She had no idea she was so unliked. Well, she didn't care much, after tonight it wouldn't matter anyway. Their behaviour only strengthened her resolve to go ahead with her plans.

After the bulk of the crowd has pushed through, the two gatekeepers reappear to help the trampled Turquoise off the ground. One of them is indeed Big John Sweeney.

Chapter 10
BLACKWORK WORK

Sarita and Elio pop their heads up just enough to see the three men fast approaching. They are nearly at the entrance to the stairway. It is now too late to try to make a run for it and being trapped in the stairwell with them is a very dangerous option. There is only one option and Sarita is not going to like it.

'Fuck. Shit. Quick, I'm sorry, Sarita, we need to hide now.' His voice rising, Elio is starting to panic. He's looking about frantically.

'What? No way am I staying here. I can barely breathe.' Sarita is not interested.

'You won't be breathing if you don't do what I say right now. These men are trouble, and we don't have time to get out. Hide now!' He is becoming more anxious and agitated by the second.

They both look around for somewhere to hide. Sarita zones in on a bundle of clothes in the corner of the floor. She dives into it, throwing them over herself, blending into the fabric jigsaw. She is gagging, now realising this is a pile of clothes waiting to be washed, not a washed pile. If Derek even washed his clothes at all. She didn't think it was possible for the smell to get worse in here but now she knows anything is possible. Did he use these clothes for toilet paper?

Elio dance-leaps across the room into Derek's wardrobe, takes a quick look towards the front door.

'Ready, Sarita, they're coming. You OK?' he whispers as loud as he dares.

'Either way I'm dying in here...' she starts, but Elio has noticed the doorknob turning, putting his finger to his lips to stop her talking.

He quickly closes the wardrobe door and waits silently in complete darkness. He can feel clothing hanging around him. There is something furry against his ankle. He was just a little less terrified of the wardrobe than who was coming through the door. He can hear it swing open, familiar voices.

'Derek, wake up. Time to get to work.' The men have entered thinking Derek is asleep and are oblivious to his condition. 'Hey, Fat Fuck. You hear me? Let's go. The gates have just opened, we've got work to do.'

Elio can hear footsteps and sounds of things being moved on the table. They walk right by him, inches from his face with only a thin piece of wood separating them. It's nerve-wracking. There are sounds of disgust and coughing coming from the men, comments about the filth and smell. Elio can hear they are going towards Derek's chair, which is not far from Sarita's clothing cave. He hopes she stays still. A new voice speaks.

'Come now, Derek, wakey wake...what the fuck? Derek? Hey, wake up.' He slaps Derek's face harder than he needs to, sending blood and dribble splatter over their legs and dripping down the vibrator. A noise that sounds like a muffled sneeze makes them all stop. One of the men holds one hand in the air, index finger up, to silence everyone. To listen. They all fall quiet, looking around the room for anything suspicious.

Sarita is quietly panicked. All these smells are starting to overwhelm her. She had no choice but to bury her pretty pixie face into the clothing to stifle her sneeze. She couldn't believe she was here right now, hiding in the shit-smelling darkness in a pile of damp, stinky clothes which she is confident are randomly covered in body fluids.

Still silent. *Tik tock...tick tock...tick tock.* A minute passes in silence. No one moves. The man who appears to be the leader bends down, his ear next to Derek's head, listening. He can hear Derek's ragged breathing, notices the vibrator in his mouth and his broken nose, the blood. Derek cough/splutters in his sleep and it appears to sate his curiosity about where the sound came from, the men accepting it was Derek.

'Someone has been here,' the leader acknowledges, 'someone who obviously wasn't a fan of Derek.' He continues his observation aloud for the benefit of the other goons.

'Broken nose and a penchant for massive purple vibrators. Somehow, I don't think Derek did this to himself. Good news is...if you can call it good news...is that our friend here is still very much alive.'

'Well, why won't he wake up, Boss?' goon junior interjects.

'I think he has been drugged, he's out cold. Fuck!' He's checking Derek's eyes, opening his eyelids but no one is home. He slams his fist on the table and swipes across it. Clutter and filthy glassware tumble to the floor with a mad smash crash. Inside the cupboard, Elio is caught off guard, startled by the ruckus. He hopes Sarita is OK.

Sarita is curled into the smallest foetal position she can manage, slightly suffocating. She is too scared to do anything, just focusing on trying to remain calm, breathe, and not have a panic attack. She can hear the breaking glass and muted angry voices. The boss speaks.

'That little rat Elio better not have anything to do with this. Dancing around, showing off, drawing attention to us. I'm sure he comes here to top up his steps. Ungrateful little prick.'

The mention of his name gives Elio a sickness in the pit of his stomach. They are clearly still angry about him going solo.

He was right to hide. They threatened to cut off his feet. His dancing feet! Sarita can hear the muffled voices. She thinks she hears Elio's name mentioned, but she can't be sure. She hopes not. Footsteps travel towards the computer.

'Either of you two know anything about this using this computer? We may not have Derek, but we've still got the tools to complete the task.' The computer flashes and beeps, as though it is acknowledging its abilities. Goon junior number two finally adds to the conversation.

'You know who would probably know how to use it? Elio. He was always smart with this kind of stuff when he worked for us.'

'Right you are. So, let's find Elio while we wait for Fat Fuck here to come back to Earth.' The boss motions to Derek, turns to goon junior one. 'Cherub, you stay here and keep an eye on Derek in case he comes around. Angel and I are going to head to the stadium, maybe Elio is hanging around there.' Cherub is not happy; he doesn't want to be the one stuck babysitting Fat Fuck and his vibrator in this sewer-scented hellhole.

'Fuck Angel, Ima go with you, Boss. Angel can stay. Ima always stuck babysitting.' He's not happy. Angel throws him a filthy look, with a little bit of 'you'll pay for this later' written across his face.

'That's because you are a baby, Cherub. You get along so well with them.' Boss is mocking in his tone, putting Cherub back in his place. 'You do as I say. You don't question my decisions. You stay.' Boss looks at him sternly, daring him to speak.

Cherub wilts into the wall.

In the wardrobe, Elio's heart sinks. Not only are they not all going to leave, but he now knows who they are for sure. Boss, Cherub, and Angel. Each have a bone to pick with him and none of them is the forgive-and-forget type. He is starting to wonder if today will be his last day. But he can't help feeling a strong sense of responsibility for Sarita. He brought her into this mess, so he has to find a way to get her out.

It was hard to be sure, but from Sarita's muffled clothing position, she thought they said they were going to leave to find Elio. She was somewhat comforted by the thought that they were finally going to leave. She allowed herself a little smile, she just had to hang in a little bit longer. She was curious how a sweet guy like Elio could be involved in something so messed up.

'Boss, should we call Turquoise? Let her know about Derek? What if we...' Angel tries, but is cut off by Boss.

'No, definitely not. Fitzenberger doesn't have to know about any of this. Besides, it makes us look unprofessional. We will sort it out. If we can't make it work in time, she can find out then, not a whisper of any of this before then. Is everyone clear?' He looks to his associates. 'Cherub? Angel?'

'Yes, Boss. We clear.' In unison, accompanied by head nodding and nervous foot shuffling by Cherub.

Elio's ears are on heightened listening at the mention of Turquoise. He did not know Turquoise even knew the gang, never mind actively worked with them. It reminds him about his earlier pickpocketing and he feels his pocket for the purse he liberated from Turquoise earlier in the day. It's still there.

'Angel, let's go. Cherub, hang. Keep an eye out for anything or anyone acting out. We still don't know for sure if it was Elio who did this to Derek so eyes and ears open. No sleeping, got it?'

Cherub is coy and humbled; he's been busted sleeping on the job before.

'Eh, Boss, you got it.' Cherub nods to Boss.

Boss and Angel make moves towards the door. A last-ditch attempt from Cherub for fresh air.

'Boss, can I wait outside?' A hopeful face.

'No, you may not.' Boss and Angel are stepping through the doorway to the stairwell, Boss leans back in for one last look at the room. His brain clicks, storing that image in his photographic memory. Just in case anything is awry when he returns, he will know exactly what has changed.

Both Elio and Sarita hear footsteps leaving and the door close. It's now silent again, except for Esme beeping and flashing away and Derek's haggard breathing.

Sarita is giving herself a couple of minutes before she emerges, just to be sure. That's if Elio does not come to get her beforehand. Elio knows that even though it is silent, Cherub is still there brooding. He hopes Sarita does not reveal herself too early, he's not sure if she is able to hear anything under the clothing. He cracks the wardrobe door open very slowly, giving him a very limited view, but Sarita's clothing cave is visible. He can't see any movement in there. He hopes she has not suffocated.

Cherub is standing by the window, the only spot with fresh air. It also allows him a vantage point to see anyone approaching. If Elio is coming, Cherub will see him first. He gazes out over the park, but no one is out. For a moment he could believe he was the only one left alive in the whole world. Everyone is now at the stadium as the evening starts to swallow the day entirely. He briefly imagines he is Will Smith in the I Am Legend movie. He'd always liked to think of himself as a tough guy with a good heart, when in reality he is an idiot clutz wreaking havoc for stolen steps.

Through the crack, Elio can see clothing starting to move, very slowly, but Sarita is definitely starting to dig her way out. He needs a plan, quick. He cannot see Cherub from his position, but he imagines he would be where any other person would be in this room, by the window. He deduces that Cherub would be looking out the window, waiting for him. There is nothing good to look at inside anyway. Elio knows he must use his opportunity, while Boss and Angel are away, to get them both out. They could overpower one goon but certainly not three. He makes his decision. It's now or never. He will reveal himself to Cherub, thus alerting Sarita of his presence.

Elio quietly and slowly keeps opening the door. He plans to take Cherub by surprise; he wants not to be choc-wedged in the wardrobe when Cherub notices him. That would put him at a massive disadvantage. Cherub could just close the door on him and lock it up till Boss and Angel returned. He would love that, what a hero. The door is almost open enough for Elio to step out when his stomach sinks.

Sarita has waited quietly in the filth for long enough. She has decided that she is going to free herself and see what's up with Elio. She rolls out of the remaining clothes onto the floor. As she goes to stand up, her movement has already caught Cherub's attention.

At the window, Cherub can hear a new ruffling noise accompanied by quiet groans. He turns his head from the window to the strangest sight of a beautiful young woman emerging from a fabric cocoon, like a beautiful butterfly. He is struggling to believe what is happening before his eyes. Is he having a stench-induced delusion? This must be a gift for him, materialising out of nowhere. He turns his body to face her.

'Well, hello there, pretty lady.' He looks her up and down hungrily. 'How long ya been here?' He is starting to drool, his tongue hanging out a bit.

'Did ya come to see me, did ya? Well, well, what ima gonna do with you?' Cherub adjusts his crotch and licks his lips. They are cracked and dry like his feet, his tongue is covered in white spots from oral thrush. 'I can think ov a few things, eh?' He is a disgusting human being.

Startled, Sarita is like a deer in the headlights. She clocks Cherub by the window ogling her in a predatory manner. She does a hard blink in the hope that when she re-opens her eyes, he will have somehow transformed into Elio. Failing that, Sarita realises she is really in trouble.

'Where'd ya come from lil lady? Huh? Huh?' Cherub snorts, 'I know where ya goin'...ya goin' with me, bitch.' He takes one step towards her.

Cherub cannot see Elio from his position so is still completely unaware of his presence. The door is ajar on the wardrobe, the opening facing away from him towards Sarita. But he's not observant enough and too swept up with Sarita to notice. Sarita starts to quickly scan the room, looking for an improvised weapon. As she sweeps her eyes across the space she sees Elio in the wardrobe, his index finger to his lips in the hush position. She casually keeps scanning, trying not to bring Cherub's attention to the wardrobe. She is feeling more emboldened now she knows Elio has her back.

She takes one step back to match every step Cherub takes towards her. She is trying to draw him past the wardrobe so Elio will be behind him. Suddenly she finds herself hard against the wall, out of backward steps. Cherub also stops.

'Where ya think ya goin'? Eh?' Cherub does a quick sidestep. Sarita reacts, sidestepping the other way. Cherub steps to the other side, causing Sarita to quickly do the opposite. Cherub laughs. He's playing cat and mouse with her.

'Little mousey, don't try to run. This is fun. I could be in for a long wait 'ere so how 'bout we take it nice and slow.' He touches his crotch. 'Bet a quality bitch like ya likes to take it slow. Nice 'n romantic. Eh? Eh?' He licks his lips again. He's clenching and unclenching his fists repeatedly and shuffling his feet, becoming restless. He still hasn't moved past the wardrobe as he enjoys taunting Sarita and having his moment. Sarita would love him to stay that far away from her, but she knows she needs to draw him closer.

'What could you possibly do to me, fuckface?' She deliberately holds her eyes on his crotch, making it known she is looking at it. 'Tickle me to death? Bet your dick fell off years ago, it's nice to have a dream though, good on you, living in hope.' She smiles a sweet, smug smile at him. Cherub can't believe she just spoke to him like that. He is the one in control here, not her. And his dick did still work, just. He is becoming enraged with his new girlfriend.

'What da fuck did ya just say to me, bitch?' He takes another step towards her. 'The fuck ya think ya are, eh? The fuck!' He kicks some empty bottles on the floor in her direction, with force. Sarita jumps, his quick step up to violence taking her off guard. One bottle smashes against the wall, narrowly missing her, only a small fragment finding its way to injure her arm with a mild cut. She still needs him to come closer. She's emboldened by his reaction.

'Oh, quick call your mummy, a little girl said something mean to big old boofhead. Waaa! Shall I call the waaambulance?' Behind the sass she is crapping herself, but a girl's got to do what a girl's got to do. Cherub's face morphs into something even uglier than he already was as he takes another step towards her. Even more incensed now, he explains how it is.

'Ya know, I was gonna take things slow and spend some time with ya, treat ya real nice, but I can tell ya don't like nice, so let's just get it going and quit wastin' time.' He takes another step, his eyes darkening, face reddening. Anger swelling inside like a shaken soda can, pressure building up ready to explode.

'Now ya makin' me real angry, I'm not nice when I'm angry, best you behave, bitch. Don't wanna end up like my last girl, do ya? Ha? Do ya? She gone now.' He was nearly there, he just had to take two more steps to move past the wardrobe. Sarita's heart is beating out of her chest, she is sure Elio must be able to hear it. She counters.

'We won't be wasting time, limp dick, pretty sure you're a 30-second wonder so we will have plenty of time...'

Something snaps in Cherub and he suddenly rushes her. Neither Elio nor Sarita are expecting the rush. Suddenly Sarita screams banshee-like as he lunges towards her, all sass gone she is now genuinely terrified of what might happen. He grabs her hair, pulling her towards him caveman style as she windmills arms over his head and shoulders. He tears out her earring with his teeth, trying to bite her.

'Elio! Elio! Help! Eli...' Before she can finish, Elio jumps on Cherub's back. His legs wrap around his waist as he plunges his thumbs as deep as possible into Cherub's eye sockets, rotating them around, trying to get behind his eyeballs. Cherub does a high-pitched, unhuman scream, releasing his hands from Sarita, swinging them back over his shoulders, trying to get the monkey off his back. He's flailing about blind, running into furniture, and smashing things. Screaming like a bobcat and skinwalker fighting. Blood starts to ooze from his eye sockets. He takes a few steps back into the wall and starts smashing his back against it, trying to shake Elio off. Elio is taking some hard hits being the buffer between the wall and Cherub's back, but he manages to keep his thumbs locked in Cherub's sockets, which now have a lot of blood running out of them. *Bang, bang!* Up against the wall, this one winds Elio, he is starting to lose strength. It is like a possum fighting a bull. Cherub, still screaming ungodly things. Elio is starting to lose against the sheer brute strength of an angry goon with bleeding eye sockets. He can't breathe squeezed between the wall and Cherub, he can't expand his chest. Elio starts to lose strength; his thumbs drop out of Cherub's sockets and his arms fall limp. Just as his vision starts to go dark, he thinks he sees some of Cherub's teeth fly across the room.

Sarita, wielding the giant vibrator by its head, smacks Cherub across the face with every bit of strength she has. A hollow *thwack!* She swings, the balls end makes contact with his face, which moves independently from his body, twisting off to the side as his teeth depart his mouth on their flight to freedom. Following them, a bloodied red trail fans out across the room. Cherub drops like a stone. He collapses onto the floor, trapping Elio's legs under his heavy torso.

The screaming has stopped. The fighting has stopped. It's suddenly deafeningly quiet as Sarita tries to catch her breath and takes stock of her surroundings. She's bent over, clutching her stomach, tears streaming down her face, chest heaving.

Cherub is well and truly out. Elio also. After the initial shock wears off, she notices Elio is trapped underneath Cherub and quickly goes to him.

'Elio? Elio?' She lightly slaps his cheeks, lowers her ear to his mouth to check his breathing. He is breathing. She tries to lift Cherub off his legs but cannot move him. Looking around she spots a broom, which she retrieves. She slips one end under Cherub's back, using the other end as a lever to lift/roll Cherub over just enough. Using her feet, she pushes Elio's legs out from under Cherub, lowers Cherub and what used to be his face back down onto the floor. She checks Elio's breathing again and rubs his legs, trying to get the circulation going.

'Elio? Elio? Wake up. Elio?' Desperate, Sarita moves up to his face. 'Elio? Please wake up.' She thinks she sees his eyelids flutter, but he isn't moving. Her heart sinks. 'Elio...please. Come back. I need you.' It dawns on her she might be alone from now on to deal with the problem she now finds herself in. She lowers her head, tears forming, but she's trying not to cry.

'Wake up...please.' She swallows hard. The silence stretches into minutes. She starts to sob quietly, her face now streaked with tears. They haven't known each other that long, but under these extreme circumstances, they have been thrown together and built a strong bond in such a short space of time. For Elio, it seems like they have already been together for ages, he has been admiring her for a while. It is so easy for them. Sarita sees Elio's chest jaggedly heaving up and down in short spasms. She places her hands on him to calm him. She's scared, wonders if he is having a seizure.

'Elio, please. Don't go. I need you.' She looks back up to his face. He's smirking, trying not to smile or laugh. Sarita is confused at first, until he speaks.

'I'm back.' He laughs bitterly. Sarita is not sure if she should be annoyed with him or elated.

'What the fuck, Elio.' She smacks both her hands down on

his chest. 'That's not funny. I thought you were dying.'

'Aw, come on.' He looks into her eyes. 'I just wanted to hear those three little words.'

'Oh, you mean I hate you?' She is softening.

'Well, to be honest, I was hoping for I love you, but I need you is also pretty sweet. I can settle for that.' He looks at her fondly. 'We can work towards the love part.'

He starts to sit up with the help of Sarita. They take a moment together, amongst the filth, the fresh blood, and teeth. Amongst the stench of shit and sweat. Amongst the two broken-faced bodies, a giant vibrator. They take a moment to embrace, be young and in lust. They finally draw back from the embrace and gaze into each other's faces again.

'Hey, nice moves, Sarita. You got him good. You saved my life. Thank you.' Elio is grateful they both came out of this relatively unscathed. Sarita looks to her attacker with disgust, puts her head down to whisper sweetly into Cherub's ear.

'Who's the mouse now, motherfucker.' She stands up and gives him a swift kick in the ribs for good measure. She'd never been violent towards anyone her whole life but found she really enjoyed the kick. It was satisfying. Elio watches her curiously as she picks up the vibrator, placing it on Cherub's chest, in his hands, with the head in Cherub's mouth. The same way they found Derek. Nice touch.

'Joke's on you, Cherub, vile little angel.' Sarita and Elio lock eyes and giggle.

Soulmates.

Sarita smells herself and instantly regrets it. 'I need a shower or six, those clothes weren't clean. I may need something stronger, like turps. Smelt like shit, sweat, and piss in that pile.'

Elio tries to make her feel like he suffered just as much.

'Well, you should try the wardrobe. Dark…damp…stinky…oh wait, there was also something furry in there and I don't know if I want to know what it is.' Curious, Sarita goes to the wardrobe and opens the door fully. Some dirty damp clothes hang from the rail but most of them are on the floor. There are only four hangers. As she pokes her head into the space, she can see bits of paper tacked to the walls and a hint of fur here and there. She bravely puts her hand in and takes a paper from the wall. As she brings it into the light it becomes clear what it is. It's a picture of Elio. Rather, a crude stained black and white copy with a red love heart scrawled around his face.

'Oh, shit.' Sarita is startled by it. 'I see I have competition.' She shows the picture to Elio. Elio is stunned speechless as he clocks the image. It's a candid picture of him in the park. Sarita rips the hanging clothes down to reveal a wardrobe full of Elio. Pictures, poetry about him, doctored photos of Elio and Derek together as a couple. Some sexual, some not. Elio is shocked into silence.

'I guess Derek is the one in the closet.' She tries to lighten the mood.

She then notices the other disturbing thing. Bits of hair stuck to some of the naked images, over their crotch areas. There are also smallish hairy triangles stuck to the wall and on the floor.

'Pass me the grabbing aid, please.' Sarita nods towards Derek's disability reaching stick leaning against the table. Elio passes it over to her. She then uses it to pick up one of the hairy things and displays it to Elio. He reels back in disgust.

'What the fuck is that...No. I don't want to know. Yes. Tell me what it is...No, chuck it back in.' Elio is torn between ignorance is bliss and needing to know. He looks at it closer.

'Pretty sure that is a merkin. Probably worn, too.' Elio can't even try to hide his horror, then concern for Sarita's health. 'Drop that merkin!' She flicks it off the stick right back into the wardrobe.

'There's more in there, there's about...' Elio cuts her off.

'Close the door, please. There are some things we don't need to know.' He scrunches up the picture of him and pockets it. No way he is leaving it here for Derek to masturbate in his merkin over.

'So, what are we going to do now?' Sarita surveys the warzone around them. Elio's legs are becoming restless again now that the blood has returned and he starts to jiggle them.

'Here and now is not the place for dancing, Elio, unless we're dancing out the door.' Sarita smiles at her own joke.

'I came here to help you, Sarita. I was going to top up your steps with Derek and Esme's help.' Elio is a bit flat and sore now his adrenaline has simmered down. Sarita softens upon seeing him deflated, but she needs to know what the hell is going on.

'What's the deal with Derek? Did you do that to him? I thought I heard those guys say you did it?' She looks him in the eyes, she needs honesty.

'No, come on Sarita, you were with me when we arrived. No, I did not. I need Derek and Esme. That would be foolish.' He's just as confused about what they walked into. 'But it clearly wasn't my old friends either. I have no idea who would have an interest in coming here and why they would do him like that.' They both look to Derek, still out of it and drooling. Their eyelines take them to Cherub, ungraciously lying on the floor missing teeth and eyes. Sarita needs to know.

'What about this really nice guy here, Cherub? And the other two guys that were here? How do you know them and why do they hate you so much?'

Elio is open and honest with her. 'I used to work for them. Harvesting steps. They're not happy that I left. I was very good at my job.' He knows they shouldn't linger longer. 'The other two are going to come back at some stage and we 100% cannot be here. We should go to the stadium, you never know, one of us might win something, at the least you can have the free dance.' He looks at Derek. 'Derek can't help us right now anyway, he is...indisposed.' Elio throws a disgusted look Derek's way, continues, 'I was hoping to help you today, but we will have to come back later, maybe even tomorrow. It's too hot right now.' He studies the computer. It flashes and beeps in response, like it is trying to tell Elio something. He adds, 'And when we do, I'm going to torch that fucking wardrobe.'

Chapter 11
THE STADIUM

Upbeat music blasts loudly, reverberating around the stadium speakers in turn, creating a delayed echo of noise. Combined with the excited chatter of thousands of people, it becomes almost impossible to think. Agnes is standing beside Aksel clutching his forearm. Rolling is now out of the question, it is jam-packed in the stadium. She checks her SLT. Already today she has walked more than she should have through part of the park and the stairs to Derek's. She grimaces a little realising she's already over her set daily allowance.

The vibe is excitement, everyone getting their annual natural high, endorphins on full throttle. The place is lit up like a city square Christmas tree. Drones make different formations in the sky, proving to be hazards to the gyro boys and the gliders. A glider went down earlier after a mid-flight fight with one, coming off second best as the drone rotor shredded his wings. He went plunging into the upper stands on the north side. No one bothered to check on him, too many steps to go up. Over time the whole community had built up a 'You chose your way, you deal with it' kind of attitude. Self-preservation was at the forefront of everyone's decision-making.

Height advantage allows Aksel to look over the vast majority of people. He's looking about, keen to see if Big John

Sweeney is actually here or if he had mistaken someone else for him. He makes his way closer to the stage, his frame providing a corridor for Agnes to follow behind without being squashed.

A slightly damaged Turquoise Fitzenberger is getting onto the stage, assisted by the two gatekeepers. Her hair is not so coiffured anymore, after the trampling. That's when Aksel spots him. It is him. It is Big John Sweeney. Aksel can't believe his eyes. He is holding Fitzenberger's hand to help steady her up the stairs. The guy is one of the biggest anti-establishment people he knows. He refuses to participate. This makes Aksel very curious and suspicious, especially since he appears to be working for Turquoise. What gives?

As she is about to start, the dastardly pogo stick gang arrives, just in time.

Thack-boiing...thack-boiing...thack-boiing.

The pogo punks, as they like to refer to themselves. They all wear garish-coloured Lycra in their gang colours, and all seem to have constantly sweaty crotches, butt cracks, and underarms. They are actually more disliked than the ballers and cause just as much carnage as them, if not more. Rude, belligerent, and a menace to society. Like balling, pogoing can present its own set of dangers to the user and those unfortunate enough to be around them. Everybody had heard about Francis K Appledix, the mechanic. He pimped his pogo big time, taking the coil spring out of the bottom and replacing it with a hydraulic spring. He could take the highest, longest jumps. He was missing for about four days, no one had heard a thing from him. Then some kids in the park noticed something large hanging high from a tall tree. Sure enough, it was Francis K Appledix. It became apparent he had come off his stick in the air and been flung into a large tree. As he fell back to earth, he got his neck caught in a V of tree branches and accidentally hung himself. He was hanging there for days. By the time they got him down, his eyes had been pecked out by birds and his lips and nose were eaten by some type of tree rodent. They loved soft tissue. His stick was found high up in the tree next to him. Sure, pogo sticks made the most of their steps, but at their own peril!

Now more of them coming. *Thack-boiing…thack-boiing…thack-boiing.* There are about 200 of them boinging around everywhere, landing indiscriminately throughout the crowd. Landing on top of people, boinging back up off people's heads and backs. Breaking necks and bones of bystanders. Karma comes very quickly for some pogo punks as they lose balance on the uneven ground of people's bodies. Losing grip and flying off their sticks like ragdolls, plunging back to the ground in various formations. There is screaming and panic. It is bedlam.

After a couple more minutes of unrest, the punks settle into their positions and get off their sticks, the chaos simmering down aside from the occasional groan of pain and crying injured.

Turquoise just watches it all. This place is lawless, and she isn't about to put the punks offside. They could make your life hell. She wasn't one for confrontation anyway. Turquoise motions to the DJ to turn the music down. The gatekeepers slink off the stage into the rooms underneath the grandstand. This is noted by Aksel, and he starts moving forwards to follow with Agnes in tow. Turquoise begins speaking.

'Good evening, my beautiful Sunshine City family!' She opens her arms in a wide hug, feigning warmth. 'Welcome to the annual Sunshine City Lottery. As you all know, we have a lot going on tonight. Some very lucky people will be given the gift of unlimited steps.' She sweeps her arm across in front of her, motioning to the whole crowd. 'Some will receive the gift of the right to procreate, without having to use your steps.' There are whistles and whoops from the crowd, some making inappropriate gestures. Thrusting their hips or making a circle with their index finger and thumb and poking their other index finger through it repeatedly. It has been a while for most, and their behaviour is all very juvenile.

Turquoise continues once the crowd has calmed down again.

'Even more exciting, somebody will be chosen to join our very important Step Handling and Integration Team.'

'SHIT!...SHIT!...SHIT!' the crowd begins to chant, irking Turquoise. It really pushes her buttons, she hates that they mock such an important group that she considers herself the leader of. Rest assured, she isn't giving that position to just anyone. She hates the general population.

'And tonight, everyone wins. Don't forget you can dance without penalty for one whole hour – our free dance.' Turquoise feels generous as the crowd whoops it up. Most people are happy just for the free dance, to be able to finally let loose without death knocking down their door. What a privilege.

As Aksel and Agnes get deeper into the bowels of the building, Turquoise's speech becomes lost and the music sounds so far away. Up ahead Aksel sees Big John and the other gatekeeper turn opposite corners, disappearing out of sight. Big John with his heavy sack strapped to the skateboard, dragging along behind him. Aksel is curious. Where are they going and what are they up to? What has he got in his sack today? Why would he work for Turquoise?

'Why are we following your friend?' Agnes whispers. For some reason, she feels she shouldn't talk aloud. 'What's going on? We will miss out on the free dance. Come on, Aksel, let's go back. It's not worth the steps.' She is tugging on the back of his t-shirt, checking her SLT yet again.

'Something's not right. I'm not sure exactly what that is at this moment, but something is definitely going down.' Aksel is jittery, looking down every hall or entrance they pass.

Constantly swivelling his head about. Wary. Now he checks his SLT again, silently wondering how many steps chasing John will use, weighing his options. It now reads 29 000 207. He bites his lip.

'Big John never comes to these types of events. He is anti-social, anti-establishment. I think he may be working for Turquoise for some reason.' They turn the corner where Big John disappeared. It's a long, curved hallway which forms a huge oval shape under the stadium. A service corridor for goods and supplies to be taken quickly to all areas of the stadium out of public view. It would usually be busy with carts of food, drinks, sports gear, and merchandise being distributed around the stadium, but not tonight. It is eerily empty. A series of random utility rooms come off the left and right sides. Big John is nowhere in sight. It is very quiet.

'Shh.' Aksel motions to keep quiet. They both creep along, poking their heads tentatively in the darkened rooms as they pass. Most are empty. Some have shelving with various boxes stacked on them. One is full of sports gear. There seems to be a costume room containing racks of elaborate headpieces, salsa/carnival style dancing clothes, mascot costumes, an unusually high amount of sequined hotpants in various colours, and 16 fake big noses, to stick over your own.

Ting, ting, ting. The sound of metal tapping on metal. It sounds like it's coming from ahead, somewhere to the left. It's hard to tell as the sound bounces around the empty spaces in the building's belly. Following is the sound of dull heavy wheels rolling along the cement floor. Aksel quickly grabs Agnes and pulls them both into the nearest room. The rolling sound is now in the main corridor. Aksel very slowly sticks his head around the corner to see Big John, wheeling his skateboard sack further away from him before disappearing into another side room. They quietly step out of the room back into the corridor and make their way towards the room Big John entered. *Ting, ting. Zzzpppt. Zzzpppt.* Aksel and Agnes edge their way towards the room of suspicious sounds. Both flat up against the wall, crab-walking like cartoon burglars, trying to minimise their shadows and size. Aksel slowly moves his head around the corner of the door to peep inside. Big John has his back to him, fiddling in his sack. *Zzzpppt.* Well-practised at working with his one good arm, he easily tears off a piece of gaffer tape and wraps it over something shielded by his body. The room is only lit indirectly by the corridor lighting, it's hard to tell what's what.

Making sure there is no one else around, Aksel quietly makes himself known.

'John…hey, John. Everything alright?' He is speaking softly, trying not to startle him. John swings around wielding a piece of pipe, his face screwed up, indecipherable. Aksel reels backwards, almost toppling over Agnes.

Chapter 12
REVELATIONS

Making their way towards the stadium, Elio and Sarita are wary. The streets are deserted, which would make it even easier for Boss and Angel to spot them travelling. They keep to the walls of buildings and underneath trees, avoiding the open roads or footpaths. Elio is piggybacking Sarita again to preserve her steps; he is way more worried about her dying soon than he lets her know. He doesn't want to panic her and for now it's a fun game for her to be carried about. She loves it. The truth is he likes doing it anyway, it feels chivalrous, and he enjoys her body heat against him. They pass the injured stiltwalker the ballers knocked over hours earlier. He's broken his leg and cracked his head coming off the stilts and is still lying in the same position, unable to help himself. He would not be making it to the stadium tonight. They do not help him; they do not want to expose themselves.

They can hear the stadium before they reach it. Loud bass throbs, leading the way like the pied piper of dance. As they get closer, they can hear the wall of noise from excited citizens. Whoops and yahoos. Except for those injured by the late arrival of the pogo punks, everyone is in a great mood. Outside the gates they can hear Turquoise's voice, distorted through the microphone and applause. The lottery is well underway, some are claiming their prizes already. Her voice triggers Elio to remember again he has her purse. Stopping outside the gate, Elio lowers Sarita from his back. He retrieves Turquoise's purse from his pocket, shows it to Sarita.

'Look. I forgot I had it. I liberated Turk-kwoises's purse from her when she passed us earlier in the streets.' He holds it up for Sarita to see. 'Now we know she is involved with Boss let's have a look in here.' He opens the purse and starts fingering through the contents, throwing items of no interest onto the ground willy-nilly. He stops at a membership card for the Bondage Babes, shows it to Sarita. They both start laughing.

'No thank you, Turk-kwoise!' He throws it to the ground, pretending it's poisonous. Elio is not exactly sure what he is looking for, but he is looking for something, a link to the goons. He'll know when he sees it. What could they possibly be doing for her?

And there it is. Elio holds up a piece of card with a number scrawled on it. There is no name, but Elio knows the number. It is his old work number and it belongs to Boss. In very small handwritten script at the bottom are the words:

harvester/jsdisposal
SHIT win/reward

He flips the card over, revealing it to be Turquoise's SHIT business card with her contact details on it.

He shows Sarita. 'What do you think this means? I heard Boss talk about Turquoise at Derek's house. They are definitely up to something with her.' He points to the number. 'See this number, I know for sure it belongs to Boss. And he is a harvester. Not sure what the jsdisposal means though.'

He's thinking for a minute, turning the card over in his hand. You could almost hear the gears in his brain shift up a notch.

'Could it be Boss is going to win the SHIT position in

exchange for whatever he has been doing?' He accentuates the looseness of the term 'win' with exaggerated middle and index finger air quotation marks. Sarita is not completely up to speed yet.

'OK, so...Are you saying that the prize of SHIT membership is rigged, and she is giving it to Boss in exchange for... whatever it is he is doing for her?' Sarita is getting it.

'That's exactly what I'm saying, Sarita. This shit is rigged. We need to find out what Boss is up to. It must be big to get this reward. It will basically make him untouchable.' He pockets the card and throws the remaining purse and contents into the nearby bins.

'OK, let's go in,' Elio instructs Sarita, 'stay close to me and be careful. I get the feeling Boss and Angel are already here looking for me. They want to chop my feet off.' He looks to his feet, smiles sadly, and starts moving inside followed closely by Sarita, walking herself this time.

'It's me...Aksel...Aksel. Remember we spoke in the street today?' He has his hands up to show he's not a threat. It takes Big John a moment to recognise him. He lowers the pipe.

'What you do Ax? Why you here?' He seems annoyed to see Aksel here. 'I said dunno go, dunno go. Why Ax? You gonna go? Gonna go?' He locks eyes with Aksel, looks to Agnes. 'You two gonna go. Take 'er, go. Go away, Ax.' Big John motions go-away hand signs. He then goes to the doorway and, paranoid, looks up and down the corridor.

While he is distracted, Aksel tries to get a look in his sack and see what he has been doing. In the half-light he can make out some pipes, two rolls of gaffer tape, plasticine, some electronic pieces with wires attached, and a small selection of tools. He probes Big John.

'Mate, that's a lot of odd things you got in your sack. What are you up to? We heard you working on our way up the corridor.' Aksel has his suspicions, but he needs confirmation from the horse's mouth.

'Ax, you gonna go?' Big John gives him nothing. He is becoming more insistent that Aksel and Agnes should leave. He pokes his head out the door and swivels it about again, like he is expecting someone any moment. Then the *click clack* of heeled shoes starts to echo down the corridor. He quickly pokes his head back in, turns to Aksel and Agnes, dead serious. He's looking about the room desperately.

'Getto hide, Ax, and 'er.' He looks to Agnes. 'Getto hide now!' He is whispering urgently. 'Fast. Now.' He is frantically looking about the room but there is nowhere to hide. It is empty aside from a few chairs and a wooden slatted bench seat. *Click clack...click clack...*getting louder as someone approaches. *Click clack...click clack...*almost at the door. Big John is starting to panic. He pushes Aksel and Agnes against the wall behind the open door. It's the only place to hide. Louder now, bearing down on them, *click clack*. Big John swings back to his bag and busies himself, back to the doorway. *Click clack*. Stops right at the doorway.

'There you are. I was wondering how far you'd got. Everything's going well, I trust?' Aksel and Agnes can't see but know it's a woman's voice. A familiar voice. Turquoise Fitzenberger. 'How many more have you got left to do? Are we on schedule, Mr Sweeney?'

John swings his body around to face her. 'Yessum, Ms Fritzenger. We on time.'

'It's Ms Fitzenberger. Not Fritzenger. If you want to be on the committee, you'll have to learn my name properly. You want to be on the committee, don't you?' She cocks her head to the side, staring down at John with contempt.

'Yessum, Ms Fritzenberg. I does wanna be on committee.' He nods his head eagerly. Turquoise can't help herself, she rolls her eyes. He is merely a dumb slave to her. He will never be on the committee.

'The English language is not your forte is it, Mr Sweeney? Hmm? But don't worry, you're plenty helpful for other tasks on the committee. If you pass this task successfully you stand an excellent chance of getting the position. You want it, don't you?' She looks at him, eyebrows raised inquisitively. Turquoise manipulates Big John. 'You know what to do if you want the committee prize...don't stuff it up.' She's more firm now in her delivery, staring him down.

He doesn't like her; he is using her too. Aksel was right, he is anti-everything. Big John has his own reasons for doing what he is doing.

'Yessum, ma'am,' is all he can manage as a fire starts inside him. He is sick of being treated like an idiot. One day no one will dare talk to him like this. He turns his back to her and starts tinkering, a cue for her to leave. Turquoise stays standing in the doorway, watching for a minute, finally she takes the hint.

'Well then, I shall come and check in with you later I suppose.' Turquoise waits for a response and is rewarded with a grunt. She keeps him onside. 'Good work, Mr Sweeney.' At that, she turns on her heels and click clacks her geranium smoked arse out of there.

Once the click clacking cannot be heard anymore, Agnes and Aksel step out from behind the door. He and Big John meet each other's eyes and hold contact.

'John, what's going on with Turquoise?' Aksel breaks the silence first. 'You working for her? You know she is the mayor, right? I thought you were really against all that stuff?' He's confused. And concerned. He may not be best friends with John, but he respects him and does not want to see people use him. The guy was harmless, unless you wronged him. John averts his eyes away from Aksel's question, returns to tinkering.

Aksel speaks again. 'What are you making there?' He takes a step forwards to look but is swiftly cut off by Big John as he spins around to face Aksel. His face is distorted and angry. His voice harsh.

'You gonna go now, Ax!' He stands up and gives Aksel a hard stare. He gets the message loud and clear, grabs Agnes' arm and starts backing out of the room.

'OK John, OK. We're going. Relax...we're going now.' They both step backwards out of the room into the corridor, too scared to take their eyes off him in his volatile state. Aksel chances himself one last look at John's sack contents on the way out.

As they retreat down the corridor, they can hear men talking, coming from the direction they are heading in. Boss and Angel are heading for the stage to see Turquoise. It's too late for Agnes and Aksel to duck into a side room as the men come into view. Everyone slows right down for a brief moment and eyeballs everyone else. They don't know each other but they all know they have no business down here unless they are up to something. Aksel and Boss lock eyes as they approach one another. Doing their best to suss the other out. As they pass side by side it's deathly quiet, the men acknowledge each other with a simple nod and keep moving. It seems they have made an unspoken gentlemen's agreement not to ask any questions and mind their own business. Aksel wonders if they are on their way to see Big John.

Sarita and Elio keep themselves as small as possible, hiding amongst the crowd. Elio is on guard, constantly keeping his eyes roving, on alert to Boss and Angel. Sarita has no idea what they look like so is of no help to stay out of harm's way. Elio has a plan. Instead of Boss and Angel finding him, he wants to find them first. That way he can discreetly keep tabs on them as they move about looking for him. He figures they will go back to Derek's at some point to see if he's awake, and of course they will find Cherub, all messed up. Right now, Turquoise is on stage doling out step-free sex prizes so Elio figures he will keep tabs on her. He feels confident Boss and

Angel will come to her at some stage, now that he has made the link there is something going on between them.

Turquoise calls the last remaining winners of step-free sex prize onto the stage. All the winners are up there now, ready for the mad dash to pick a partner. Men on one side, women on the other. Sarita can't help noticing all the winners seem quite young and good looking, aside from horny Norman, Turquoise's creepy younger brother. He has no redeeming qualities, short with a hook nose that never stops running, a barely-there combover, and a personality to match a rat trap. Horny Norman Fitzenberger always seemed to 'win' free sex lotteries as Turquoise vainly tried to keep the Fitzenberger gene relevant. Interestingly, Sarita wonders if maybe this competition is also rigged. Selecting the youngest, healthiest, best-looking specimens among the population for best breeding practices. That is, aside from Turquoise enabling her creepy brother to have sex with young ladies.

Brrrrrrtt! The horn sounds and the games begin. Knowing they have only a one-hour window to have sex, the winners disregard their usual step-preserving gaits and run to each other. They madly try to get their first choice of the opposite sex to go with them. It's a form of its own lotto, really. If you wait too late to accept someone, you may be left at the bottom and be stuck choiceless with whoever else is left there also. Some poor young lady was unfortunately destined to have sex with horny Norman if she got too picky. He had random offspring everywhere thanks to his sister. They were all ugly. The world did not need any more baby Normans.

Elio keeps a close eye on Turquoise as she exits the stage during the pandemonium of partner picking. As she uses the stairs, a hand extends to help her. It's Boss. With Angel, like a lap dog, by his side.

'Ha! Got them. Look, Sarita, that's Boss and Angel. They were the other two men at Derek's place. Keep your eyes on them. They're looking for me so if we know where they are we will be safe.' Elio needs her to be on high alert, both their lives depend on it. 'Remember those faces, they are bad men, Sarita.' Sarita zones in on them like a missile to a target, her eyes steely. She already hates them for leaving her no option but to hide in Derek's filthy clothes earlier and for endangering her with Cherub.

'All we need to do is avoid them,' Elio adds, 'can't be that hard.' The last part more to himself than Sarita. They can see Boss and Angel talking intensely with Turquoise, looking out over the crowd, scrutinising. Elio instinctively ducks, pushing Sarita down with him even though Boss and Angel have no chance of spotting him in the darkened crowd. He looks down at his feet. He likes his feet; they are helpful for things like walking and dancing. He really doesn't want to part with them. He looks back up just in time to see the goons disappear into the service corridor under the building with Turquoise. Elio and Sarita follow from a safe distance.

Aksel and Agnes, still in the corridor, stop to listen. They can't hear anyone talking to Big John and the footsteps have faded out. Every now and then some of Big John's tinkering can be heard filtering through the corridor. It is hard to pinpoint the location as the sound bounces around the empty space. They were sure the men had gone. Aksel isn't ready to leave yet. His need to know why Big John is acting so strange is still unresolved. He's no expert but it looks like John has the ingredients of an improvised explosive device, or IED, in his sack. Encountering the strange men added another layer to the cake of curiosity.

Agnes has had enough sneaking about. She missed out on the sex lottery already. She could have been called up to the stage for all she knew. She could be having sex right now but instead she is still entombed in the building's belly with Aksel. If you're not there at the time they draw names, they simply draw someone else's name and get on with it.

'Can we please go back out with everyone else now. Please,' she pleads with Aksel. Agnes looks up and down the corridor, 'I'm not comfortable here, I don't like this place. It's...weird.'

'I don't like it either, Agnes, but please just give me a bit more time. Something big is going down, I can feel it.' Aksel looks up and down the corridor again, weighing up his options. 'Something is not right. Give me 15 then we are gone. I will get you to that free dance, Agnes, you have my word.'

Agnes sighs. Aksel has helped her a lot today, she decides she can do this one thing for him.

'OK, fine. I'll give you fif...'

She is cut off by Aksel whispering, 'Shh. Did you hear that?' He cocks his head, moving it left to right, ears tuning in like a parabolic antenna. Right index finger raised in the air like a student seeking a teacher's attention. No one moves for a few seconds and there it is. The distinct *click clack* of heels they heard earlier. This time they are accompanied by voices. Men's voices. Aksel deduces it could only be the shady men he passed earlier, and he does not want to be seen by them again. He grabs Agnes.

'Quickly, in here.' He points to the room with the costumes in it. 'Places to hide in here.' They quickly but quietly make themselves disappear into the room behind a full rack of salsa dancing costumes. Aksel explains, 'I don't think we should let those men know we are still here. I'm getting heavy vibes from them.'

The click clacking and talking get louder as the group gets closer to the costume room. Aksel thinks he hears John's name mentioned. They are approaching the room where Aksel and Agnes are hiding, then stop directly in front of the doorway. Agnes instantly stiffens and clenches her teeth, anxious. She is sure they can hear her teeth grinding. She feels sick and scared. Almost as though he senses her heightened state,

Aksel carefully moves his hand over, placing it on her shoulder to comfort her. They look at each other, the fear undeniable in her eyes.

'So, are we clear on the outcomes tonight, gentlemen?' Turquoise looks from Boss to Angel, back to Boss. She speaks in a low tone. 'Make sure Mr Sweeney disappears tonight after his work is done. Your choice of method, but don't let him leave the building. He will be collateral damage with the rest of them once the stadium blows up after the free dance. No one will know any different.' Boss and Angel nod in compliance. Turquoise continues. 'Anyway, everyone that remains will be happy he's dead after they all find out he prepped the stadium with explosives.' She says this so matter-of-fact, dismissing the fact she is the one behind him doing so.

'It will happen, Ms Fitzenberger, you have our word.' Boss is more than happy to eliminate anyone who dares to stop him from getting onto the SHIT committee. He has his own agenda that does not involve Turquoise or Angel. Or Cherub. Or Big John Sweeney. Like most people, he doesn't even like Turquoise. He thinks she is an over-privileged, over-coiffured snob who needs to be bought down a peg, but he can play the game. He can play very well.

'Before that, Angel and I must go to check in with Derek.' He eyes Angel to go with him on this. 'Ensure that he is ready for the mass harvesting tonight. It's going to be busy.'

'I thought you would have already checked on Derek. It's getting late. We can't afford any mistakes tonight.' Turquoise speaks in a tone as though telling off a naughty child, looking from Boss to Angel, unimpressed.

'We were on our way, Ms Fitzenberger. Just though we would check in with you first as a matter of priority.' Boss is trying his best not to just knock the bitch out. He's making her feel important and it's working. She changes tone.

'Right, well, thank you for ensuring all was well here. I think tonight is going to be a great night for all of us.' She steps towards the costume room door, swings it open a bit more, bringing with it a shaft of filtered light from the corridor. Agnes and Aksel flinch, eying each other warily. 'There are plenty of costumes here if you'd like a disguise,' Turquoise continues, 'we have salsa carnival themed dancers out there tonight, you can blend right in.'

Angel pokes his head in and has a quick look around. Agnes and Aksel can see him in the light of the doorway, but Angel can't see them behind a full rack of salsa clothes topped with elaborate headpieces. Agnes is sure he is looking right at them, sure he can hear her heart pounding out of her chest, but Aksel calms her, confident they remain unseen. Angel takes his head back into the corridor to join the others.

'Good to know. We will return when we get back from Derek's. We will take care of Sweeney, you have my word.' Boss does all the talking.

'Very well. Speaking of Mr Sweeney, I better go check in with him again.' Her tone is a burden. 'He should be finished laying the explosives by now, if the dumb oaf hasn't gotten lost.' She just could not miss an opportunity to show her superiority over anyone, even a common street hustler. Boss knew he was going to have to deal with Sweeney anyway, but it still rubbed him the wrong way to hear Turquoise's superior attitude flare up again.

'I've had enough walking today.' Turquoise shuffles her feet. 'I'm not used to it and my feet are sore. I'm using too many steps.' She couldn't bring her throne carriers down here; they weren't privy to her plans, nor did her plans include them. 'Can you carry me to find Mr Sweeney?' She looks to Boss and Angel, whose faces give away their response before they can answer. They decline politely to be her slaves, citing urgency to get to Derek's.

'We really got to get to Derek's now so we have time to come back and deal with Sweeney.' Leaving her no room to protest. 'Goodbye, Ms Fitzenberger, we shall see you at the end of the night.' With that, Boss and Angel continue their exit from the building as Turquoise drags her sore feet in the other direction to find Big John. *Click clack, click clack.*

Elio and Sarita have quietly tailed Boss, Angel, and Turquoise and lay in wait for them all to leave. They see the men emerge and head towards the stadium exit, but Turquoise is not with them. Elio is confident the goons are on their way back to Derek's, but where did Turquoise get to? He and Sarita head towards the underground corridors the goons exited from to see what she is up to.

First thing they notice is how deathly quiet it is in there.

'Strange. This service corridor should be busy right now but there is not a soul to be seen. Where's the personnel, the food, the drinks, the merchandise?' Elio observes.

'I don't like it. It feels like a set-up or something. But for what?' Sarita looks around warily. 'They are not expecting us, are they?' She's concerned about her safety. She's had a rough day.

'We've come this far, we know we are safe from Boss and Angel, for now.' He grabs Sarita's hand, wonders about her expiring steps and briefly considers carrying her, but it would be too hard while trying to remain quiet.

'Let's go see what Turquoise is up to.' He takes her hand as they start walking deeper into the bowels.

Now sure that all parties have gone, Aksel pokes his head slowly into the corridor, looking left and right. He cups his hand around his ear, scanning up and down the space.

'We're clear. Everyone has gone.' He comes back to Agnes, who is now lying on the ground.

'I haven't walked this much in one day for a long, long time. Everything aches.' She explains her position to Aksel.

'It's way more comfortable for me to lie down.' Her adrenaline has also dropped, leaving her spent and tired. Aksel understands, but knowing what they overheard, time is of the essence. Agnes checks her tracker again and lets out a big sigh. 31 004 784 steps remaining. This day is really starting to add up.

'I'll give you one minute of grace then we must make tracks, Agnes. We need to find John and get him to stop this madness. He is fitting the stadium with explosives.' Aksel can't believe the way this day is going. Saying that sentence makes him shake his head in disbelief.

'Sounds like we are going to be blown up tonight, how very...cosmopolitan of Turk-kwoise.' Agnes is well and truly over it now. Against his own set rule, Aksel checks his SLT again also, fully aware that finding John will be taking from his lifespan. Considering his position now, and the possibility of being blown up tonight, he is starting to care a whole lot less about wasting steps.

He starts fingering through the costumes on the rack.

'We should put some of these on. When those two thugs return, I don't think they should see us again. They were already suss on us, it could be trouble.' He pulls out a skirt and holds it against himself for size.

'Yep, definitely that one, the colour is so amazing on you. Unless they have something shorter, you've got the legs for it.' Agnes stifles a small giggle.

Sarita thinks she can hear a very faint female giggle from ahead somewhere. She stops.

'Did you hear that?' She stops Elio, holding him back by his arm, whispering, 'I thought I heard someone giggle.'

They are both completely still, playing a game of statues with only themselves as competitors. Another small giggle emanates through the corridor.

'That must be Turk-kwoise,' Elio is whispering, 'who else

could it be, there's no one else down here.'

'What are we going to do with her?' Sarita is unsure of their next move but hopes it doesn't involve more violence or anything with an ungodly smell.

'We have to find out what she's up to. Whatever it is, if she is working with Boss and Angel, it's bad news.' He takes a tentative step forwards. 'Come, Sarita. Be brave. She's an old woman and there are two of us. If we can take Cherub, we can take her.' He takes another step, speaking lower now. 'And we have the element of surprise on our side. Shh, quietly.'

They tiptoe their way up the corridor towards the sound, stopping before every random room on the way to listen, ensuring the rooms are clear of people before moving onto the next one.

Elio cocks his head. He hears a man's chuckle this time and it sounds close. They are almost upon the sound, approaching cautiously. There's low talking coming from a room close by. More stifled giggles and chuckles. Whoever it is, is trying to be quiet.

The more Elio hears, the more convinced he is that this is in fact not Turquoise at all. They sound too upbeat and nice to be her. Turquoise never laughs, her face would probably crack right off. If she did, it must be in the privacy of her own home because no one has ever heard her. Elio allows himself a moment to imagine what her laugh would be like. Like a cackling witch, he thinks to himself, bringing a smile to his face. Sarita looks to him, eyebrows raised, wondering why he is smiling right now. They both visibly relax more upon hearing the easy, casual exchange in the room ahead. It's in hushed tones but they can feel a lightness coming from it. Not so anxious now, they approach the doorway.

For a short moment, Agnes and Aksel forget about the looming potential deaths of everyone present that night and enjoy playing dress-ups. Agnes is adjusting her headpiece when she notices a shadow fall across the doorway. She stops, signs to Aksel to be quiet and turnaround. He turns slowly as the shadow gets bigger, decides to take control of the situation. He approaches the door, planning to take whoever it is off guard. It is clear their earlier banter has given them away, he now feels stalked.

Elio and Sarita are just outside the door. It has suddenly fallen very quiet inside, alerting them to the chance it's now known they are there. Elio decides to take control of the situation, stepping up to the doorway quickly, hoping to trap whoever is inside, giving him the upper hand.

Aksel runs to the doorway to see what's happening at the same time as Elio does.

Smack!

They both bounce off each other in the doorway and fall backwards onto the floor. Aksel's skirt flips up, exposing his underwear. Both the girls are stunned, each taking a step back, trying to take everything in as the two men wiggle around on the floor. Elio and Aksel recover quickly, both in fight-or-flight mode. They jump back up, stumbling into defensive positions. Both parties have enough situational awareness to not start yelling loudly at each other, it is clear everyone was trying to keep quiet beforehand. The two men start scream whispering at each other.

'Who are you? Why did you sneak up on us?' Aksel demands. Elio puts his hands in the air, signalling he is not a threat. He looks up and down the hallway, nervous. This prompts Sarita and Aksel to do the same.

'We mean no harm,' Elio whispers, looking up the corridor again. 'Please, can we come into your room?'

Aksel is unsure. He looks over to Agnes for her input. She shrugs her shoulders. She's not getting any evil vibes from them. They almost seem as desperate as Aksel and Agnes to not be seen. Agnes and Sarita hold each other's gaze for a moment, then the penny drops for Agnes. This is the couple Agnes passed in the street earlier today, her riding his back. The couple that prompted her wistfulness. Now she can't help feeling some affinity with them, she gives Aksel the head flick of approval to bring them in.

They enter the room with their hands still in the air. Aksel motions for them to stand against a wall.

'You can drop your hands.' Aksel sees no threat here now.

Elio and Sarita put their arms to their sides. Sarita visibly exhales, puts her hands to her chest, and briefly closes her eyes.

'Thank you.' She's looking at Agnes when she says it. Agnes nods her acknowledgement.

It's only then Sarita and Elio notice what Agnes and Aksel are wearing. They are both donning brightly coloured rah-rah skirts, sequinned mesh bodices with decorative bra tops, and fruity headpieces a la Carmen Miranda. It's absurd given the circumstances. Sarita and Elio are like school kids in trouble, trying not to smile at them. Aksel starts the big questions.

'I believe you mean us no harm as we mean you no harm. Can we agree on this?' He looks to Elio and Sarita as they nod in agreement. Elio tries to explain their presence.

'Something is going down here tonight; we are trying to work it out. We've been following some gang types who seem to be working for Fitzenberger.' Keen to settle Aksel, he pulls out Turquoise's business card and shows Aksel. 'Look at this, I found it in Turk-kwoise's purse.' Aksel takes it from his hand and scrutinises the back.

'This looks like a contact number. Harvester/jsdisposal, SHIT win/reward.' He flips it over. 'This is Turk-kwoise's business card. What does this mean? What's a harvester? What's jsdisposal?' He pronounces it like one made-up word: jiz-dis-po-sal.

'I can help with some of that,' Elio offers. 'I know whose number this is, his name is Boss and he is bad news. He's a black market worker who's not afraid of a little violence to get what he needs.' He looks down at his feet longingly. 'They may be looking for me also. We've been tailing them tonight and saw them come in here with Turk-kwoise. That's why we are here now.'

He realises they don't know each other's names yet and is trying to build trust. 'I'm Elio.' He turns to Sarita. 'This is my girlfriend, Sarita.'

Sarita blushes slightly. Seems it's official, she has a boyfriend now.

'Hi.' She waves one hand shyly. Aksel reciprocates.

'I'm Aksel, and this is my friend, Agnes. We are also here following someone, someone who we believe is working for Turk-kwoise. Do you know Big John Sweeney? You've probably seen him around, he's fairly distinctive.' Aksel uses his hands to show size. 'He's about this tall, pretty solid-built guy, always has a sack on a skateboard he drags around with him. One good arm, one limp one?'

Sarita pipes up. 'I've seen that guy, he likes to hang out around the city. I wonder what happened to his arm. And what's on the skateboard? He always keeps it covered up.'

'Yeah, you will usually see him in the city,' Aksel confirms, 'but we found him down here, he's laying explosives.'

Elio and Sarita look at each other, stunned.

'Explosives? For what? Are they having fireworks tonight? I thought it was a drone show?' Sarita can't get her head around it.

'Not exactly fireworks, no.' Aksel updates them on what he knows. 'We overheard Turk-kwoise talking to some men in the corridor just before. They were clearly working for her too.' He lays it on the table. 'Her plan is to blow up the stadium at the end of the free dance, and whoever she was talking to is also tasked with getting rid of John after he has laid the explosives. One of them referred to the other as Angel.'

Elio puts it together. 'Boss and Angel, who we are following.'

'Well, they've gone to some guy called Derek's house to arrange a mass harvesting or something like that,' Aksel updates Elio.

Elio has a moment inside his own head, realising what is happening.

'And then they can harvest everyone's unused steps...' Aksel, Agnes, and Sarita all look his way.

'That's it! That's the plan.' It's a eureka moment for Elio. 'She's going to blow up the stadium tonight, everyone will die, including your friend John...jsdisposal...they're going to dispose of him after he does their dirty work.'

'Yeah, I heard them talking about John. Something about making sure he is in the stadium when it blows. Dead or alive.' Aksel gets it now. 'Get rid of the evidence, hey. Nice moves. I bet John doesn't know about this part. He thinks he's winning the SHIT position.' Aksel purses his lips.

'I used to work for these guys, but I haven't for a while,' Elio continues. 'The way it works is any unused steps from people tonight will be re-invested, or harvested, if you prefer, back into the main frame. Then the steps can be re-distributed among the survivors to lengthen their lives.'

'But how? How can one steal steps?' Aksel needs to know more.

'That's why they are going to Derek's place. He is an evil, stinky genius who has a computer he built from scratch, made especially for harvesting and uploading steps. Somehow, he has engineered his computer to offset the DNA sequence and disable the nanobots that govern our lifespan.' Elio almost spits it out, like he's eaten something rotten. He looks at Sarita who can't help herself.

'Derek's in love with Elio.' Elio throws her a disgusted look.

'Hang on.' Agnes is struck with coincidence. She looks at Aksel. 'That so-called party we went to earlier in the day, wasn't his name Derek?'

'Now that you say it, I think it was.' Aksel rolls his eyes

upwards as one does when thinking.

'He was fat and stinky, I'm not sure about genius, but he did have a big computer,' Agnes confirms. 'He called it...Elsie.'

'No, it was Esme.' Aksel corrects.

Sarita and Elio lock eyes in agreement.

'That's him! That's Derek! Did you say you went to his party?' Elio knows exactly what sort of party Derek likes to host. 'You must be the two from the park! Did he throw paper planes at you?' Elio is animated by this co-incidence and revelation.

'Yeah, he did. How do you know?' Aksel is intrigued.

Elio takes his time, not sure about how much of his activity with Derek to give away.

'I caught him throwing planes when I arrived. It's what he does to lure people in. He can't physically leave the apartment to meet his victims, so he brings them to him.'

'What do you mean victims? Us?' Agnes is quick.

'Potentially, yes. He got you there, didn't he? Did he insist on giving you a drink?' Elio knows Derek's agenda.

'Yeah, really insistent,' Agnes replies. 'Too insistent.'

'You obviously didn't drink it, or you wouldn't be standing now. He usually uses a strong dose of temazepam,' Elio elaborates. 'You drink the drink, pass out, or die if you've had too much.' Aksel and Agnes both look at each other alarmed. Elio continues, 'Then Derek harvests your remaining steps for his personal step bank. That's the scam.'

The depth of danger in their situation with Derek hits Agnes and Aksel now. They sub-consciously move closer together, Agnes wrapping her arm around Aksel's.

'Well, fuck,' is all Aksel can muster. 'You try to be nice...'

'We gave him the drink instead.' Agnes remembers, she's excited. 'Aksel gave him a big whack across his nose with his giant vibrator. It's purple.' She's animated now. 'Knocked him clean out, then he gave Derek the drink.'

'We found him knocked out, gobbing a giant vibrator!' Sarita joins in, enthralled by all this. She starts whisper giggling. 'The vibrator was on.'

'You did that?' Elio chimes in. 'That really threw my day. I mean I can't think of a more deserving and funnier outcome for Derek, but that has really fucked things for tonight. Nothing we can't do later though, I guess. Well done.' He looks at Sarita, explaining. 'I took Sarita there to upload more steps.' The tone has become more sullen, as Sarita and Elio gaze into each other's eyes and weave their fingers together, the reminder of her uncertainty written across both their faces. 'Don't worry, beautiful, we'll go back tomorrow when he's awake again,' Elio reassures.

'What about my steps? Are they going to run out?' Sarita is becoming more paranoid about her step count now she is no longer living blind.

'It's too risky to go back tonight, Sarita. I'll carry you whenever I can.' He breaks his gaze to look at Agnes and Aksel. 'You two are welcome to come too. I can also help you.'

Chapter 13

BACK AT DEREK'S DOUCHE DEN

'What the fuck is going on here?!' Straight away Boss knows something is up, he sees the door in a different position to how he left it. He and Angel survey the room. Boss doesn't need his photographic memory to know that someone has been here since they left. The proof is right in front of them. They both look at Cherub on the ground, looking even more pathetic than the last time they saw him. Missing teeth, his face a mess, eyeballs half bulging out of crimson pools, more blood splatter, and the vibrator that used to live in Derek's mouth is now parked in Cherub's. And he's pissed his pants just to top it off.

There is no improvement on Derek, he is still out like a broke prostitute. Although he is still making non-sensical gurgling noises, so he is still alive. For now, he is as useless as tits on a bull. Finally, being a big boy has worked in Derek's favour, it would take a lot of temazepam for him to not come back to the land of the living. But for now, Derek still sleeps.

'That little fuckwit Cherub.' Boss turns to Angel. 'One job. One fucking job unsupervised and this happens.' He's pissed, gives Cherub a little kick to the ribs just because. 'He didn't even have to do anything but keep watch. Fucking cocksucker useless waste of space. We should harvest his motherfucking steps.' Boss is extremely upset with Cherub's efforts today.

Cherub is asleep. Like Derek, he is making weird breathing sounds. Like he is asleep but in pain. However, unlike Derek, he isn't drooling, except for out of his eye sockets. He isn't quite as out of it as Derek.

'Let's try wake his lazy arse up.' Angel moves to the sink and fills a mouldy plastic jug with water. He moves over to Cherub and dumps it in one go, right onto his face. Cherub has waterboarded a few unlucky people in his time and now it's time to experience it for himself. His body starts rejecting the water pouring in from his nose and mouth, Cherub starts spluttering and coughing, drowning lying down. His eye sockets fill up. He is still kind of out to it as his body starts involuntarily heaving in tune with the coughing and spluttering. He finally starts to come round. Boss encourages him with another kick to the ribs.

'Wake up, dickhead!' He motions to Angel to go and refill the water jug. 'Get your pathetic arse up and explain yourself right now!' His patience is very, very thin. Thinner than nylon stockings.

Splash! Another jug is dumped unceremoniously on Cherub. Up until this point he is still having a lovely dream about raping Sarita. This jug seems to have more effect as he tries to blink himself awake, unsure why his eyes feel...distant. He rolls onto his side to stop himself drowning. He's coughing water out of his mouth, and it oozes from his nose in a viscous mixture of water and snot. It's even coming out his eye sockets. He's finally awake enough to realise he's in trouble, only just making out Boss and Angel looming over him. Angel wielding an empty jug and Boss' jaw bulging as he clenches and unclenches it, his eyes narrowed. Angel throws the empty jug in his face as he tries to sit up.

'Owee! Mam, why ya mo mat?' He's talk-moaning, spluttering, attempting to look around. His speech is even harder to decipher as he adjusts to talking with fewer teeth. Boss stares at him with disdain, then shifts his eyes to the vibrator. Cherub's eyes kind of follow him, even though they appear to be looking in different directions, shame clouding his face.

'Cherub, you dumb fuck. What the fuck is this? You had one fucking job! Get up!' Boss kicks him again, leaving him to fall back over like a frumpy rag doll. The reality of his situation has now fully hit him, and Cherub quickly scrambles to get back up. He is like a bug on its back, flailing away, which looks ridiculous and angers Boss even more. He looks pathetic.

'Owee!' As Cherub starts to lever his body up again, he puts his hand down on something sharp.

He lifts his left hand to see two of his teeth embedded in it. One with his prized gold filling.

'Sozy, Boss,' he slurs, 'somones wer ere...somones hidin.' He points to the pile of clothes on the ground. 'She in ere, unna da clof.' He's desperately trying to explain himself, but his mouth is still non-compliant. It is swollen and red, complete with fresh blood oozing down his chin.

'Unna der.' He continues to frantically point at the clothing pile. Angel walks over to it, picks up a pair of pants from it then quickly drops them, reeling backwards, almost falling over the rubbish on the floor.

'There's nothing there. It fucking reeks.' Angel's face is distorted. 'It can't be healthy being in this room.' He takes some steps back from the pile towards the window. Cherub tries again.

'A girl, hidin inther.' His speech is slowly improving as he gets used to his new mouth. 'Hidin inther clofs.' He's pointing at the pile again. Boss cottons on to what Cherub is saying. In his profession, over the years, he has mastered the language of injured goon.

'Was there someone hiding in the clothes, Cherub?' Cherub nods madly. 'A girl, did you say?' He nods even faster. 'So,' Boss continues, 'what you're saying is a girl did this to you? A girl came out of the clothes and beat you up?'

Cherub blushes, dropping his eyes to the ground. He can't look Boss in the eyes after he puts it that way.

'I ad er, I did.' He looks back to Boss. 'I ad er...somon jump my back. Sqush me eyes.' He points at what's left of his eyes dramatically. 'Th bitch,' he says more to himself than Boss.

Running out of patience with the jabbering fool, Boss tries to wrap up the story.

'Someone jumped on your back? There were two people?' Boss holds up two fingers to be clear. 'So one of them, a girl, came from the clothes.' Cherub nods again. 'And another person jumped on your back while you had the girl? Is this correct?'

'Yes, Boss, is right.' Cherub is relieved to finally get them to understand.

'Was the second person a man?' Boss questions.

'Ye. Was man,' Cherub remembers. 'Elio.' Now he really has Boss' attention.

'Did you say Elio? Did you see him?' Boss, talking faster.

'Nom, didn see im. Es on my back. Squishn me eyes.' Cherub explains. 'She call im Elio.'

'Fuck!' Boss explodes. 'Fuck...fuck...fuck!' He smashes his fist on the table with each fuck given.

'Where is he? Who was he with? Where did they go?' He wants answers now.

'Dunno er. Shez cute tho.' Cherub touches his crotch. 'I ad im too...then she whack me out.'

Fortunately for Cherub, looks can't kill or he would have died on the spot. Boss gives him a hard, judging, 'you're a piece of shit' staredown.

'Fuck you, Cherub. You can stay here. You fucking useless piece of trash.' Boss looks at Angel. 'Angel and I need to go back to the stadium and deal with John Sweeney. I bet that's where the little prick Elio has gone. Hopefully he's with his violent lady friend. Fucking stay here.' He hands Cherub a gun. 'If they come back, you know what to do. Elio has caused enough fucking drama.'

With that he turns for the door. Angel, ever faithful, close behind. Boss takes another photo with his brain to file away for their return.

Chapter 14
ACTION/INACTION

The now united team of Agnes, Aksel, Elio, and Sarita are all adding finishing touches to their salsa carnival costumes. Given everything that's going down tonight, their spirits are high. Buoyed by extra company, their burden feels lighter and they are whisper giggling at each other's outfits as Elio adjusts his sequinned G-string, repeatedly pulling it from his butt crack only for it to instantly snap its way back into place.

'How do you girls do this?' he questions.

Everyone is donning carnival face masks to hide themselves as best they can. They have all been seen already. If they get seen down here again by Turquoise or the goons, they could not just allow them to walk on by as happened earlier. That would be way too much coincidence for them to be comfortable with. Aksel is plumping out his bra top with socks and underwear. They are just about ready to go back outside for the free dance when a rumbling, rolling sound begins to emanate throughout the hallway, accompanied by the low tones of people talking. Everyone freezes, cocking their heads towards the doorway. A man's deep voice and a woman's scratchy voice. The deep voice sounds submissive and the woman's voice sounds like she is lecturing. As they get closer it becomes apparent who they are. Turquoise and Big John Sweeney.

'Maybe it's not Turquoise. What's happened to her shoes?' Agnes notes the lack of click clacking that usually warned of an incoming Turquoise. Aksel looks to her in agreeance. Weird. They are getting closer. But it is Turquoise, she's telling John what to do as they get closer to the costume room. The drag of his skateboard is heavy, even though most of the items that were in there have now been distributed throughout the belly of the stadium.

'Then after that, Mr Sweeney, you can wait for me at the entrance to the stage for the finale.' She is setting up John to stay in the stadium somewhere she can send Boss to find him easily and incapacitate him. Just to make sure he is still here to be blown up by his own explosives. She'll be long gone by then.

'Mr Sweeney, are you paying attention? This is very important. When we meet there, I will make the announcement that you have won the committee prize.' She smiles a big fake smile at him. She makes John sick inside but he goes with it, smiling back.

'Yessum, Ms Fitzgerger. Thanks. I be waitin' by 'em stairs. Waitin' for you.' He flashes his crooked, yellowing teeth. It's almost menacing.

As they pass by the costume room, Aksel notices John is now dragging Turquoise behind him on his skateboard, her heels in John's working hand. What a piece of work she is.

Soon they physically disappear in the curve of the corridor, their verbal interaction disappearing not long afterwards. The last thing they hear is the heavy, complaining, strained drag of John's skateboard, carrying more weight than it should.

Everyone remains silent and listens for another minute, just to be sure.

'Right then, let's get going to the dance. We've got to keep tabs on John so we can help him out in time.' Aksel speaks first.

'Yeah, and everyone keep a look out for Boss and Angel, they should be easy to spot. They'll be the only people not smiling or dancing.' Elio smiles. 'I'm confident Cherub hasn't made it back with them. He was unconscious when we left, his was face pretty messed up.'

Completely dressed now with a clear path to get out, they start to make their way out from the costume room into the corridor, everyone remaining as quiet as they can. Agnes grabs her coat, rolls it up tight and carries it under her arm. She will need it later to protect her while rolling. They start walking towards the exit, out to the stadium grounds, when they see Boss and Angel walking towards them from the way they are heading. They've been spotted and it's too late for any evasive action. Elio quickly grabs Sarita and spins her under his arm, leaning her backwards into him. Agnes and Aksel give him a funny look and Elio eye rolls towards incoming Boss and Angel. Aksel quickly grabs Agnes and does the same, everyone now pretending they are performers practising their dancing en route to the dancefloor. Aksel ramps it up.

'That's a two-step, Jaunita.' He pretends to be directing Agnes, making out like they are real dancers.

Sarita starts to hum a jaunty salsa tune for them as she and Elio continue to dip and whirl.

Elio is becoming more nervous as Boss and Angel get closer. Neither of them talk, they both just stare straight ahead at the oncoming dancers. Very serious, very ominous.

Elio wants to shrink as small as possible. Even though he has a mask on he is paranoid that if Boss looks into his eyes, he will know it's him. It's hard to hide fear. He is not confident they haven't already been identified; Boss may be playing dumb until he's within strangulation reach. Elio never underestimates Boss. He is smart. It's not an overly wide corridor so the two parties will pass by each other fairly closely. The foursome keeps making little dancing comments until they are finally about to pass Boss and Angel. Elio can't do it; in that moment he grabs Sarita again and whirls her around, timing it so he does not have to make eye contact with Boss as he spins away in the other direction. Boss and Angel, however, have no problem holding eye contact with Agnes and Aksel as they pass. Aksel tries to keep casual, engaging in conversation with Agnes. Boss isn't sure what to make of this odd situation, he thinks it is just dancers coming out late, but he still gives them an intimidating stare down just in case. He just likes people to be scared in his presence. He loves the power.

They finally pass each other, Boss and Angel turning their heads to keep their gaze locked on as long as possible. It takes everything Elio has to not turn around and look at them as they retreat. He knows Boss will already be doing that to them. They keep on moving forwards.

They did not see Boss and Angel disappear into the costume room.

Outside the tunnels and back to the outdoors, the fearful yet fearless foursome is pumped full of adrenalin. They're excitable and all start talking at the same time.

'I thought he was going to know it was me, for sure.' No one is more relieved than Elio. 'That's why I started dancing. I had to move.'

'Holy dirtbags! Was that Boss and Angel?' Sarita has put a face to the voices from Derek's.

'Let's go, let's go...' Agnes wants to keep moving away from danger.

'That was close. Where's John?' Aksel is scanning around the throb of people dancing. He notices Turquoise pushing through the crowds, heading towards the stadium exit. He points at her.

'There goes Turquoise, saving her own arse.' It's said with contempt.

'Don't worry. She'll get hers. Karma can be a bitch to a

bitch.' Elio watches her struggle through the crowd.

There are now salsa carnival dancers on stage leading the crowd into raptures of movement. The vast majority of people are dancing carefree, enjoying this one hour of being able to move as one likes. However, a few are too forever physically altered from years of adjusting their bodies to unnatural formations to return to their normal gait. These people look uncomfortable, like they are having a seizure.

The music is throbbing through massive speakers, their grilles vibrating violently, threatening to come loose. Lasers, in synchronicity with the music, point and slice through the night's hazy smoke-filled air like lightsabres. A strobe light is sending a group of girls into a frenzy, their limbs moving impossibly in every direction at once under its influence. Drones are making sparkling formations above, weaving and circling to morph from an animated caterpillar into a butterfly. Everywhere people are intoxicated by the music, at this point it's the only thing that matters to them. It's as though everyone has taken ecstasy. Everyone has a permanent big smile across their face. The feeling is love, joy, and happiness. People don't get much chance to experience true bliss anymore.

It will be short-lived though. Out of those who come away with no wins tonight, SHIT research has shown that after the free dance, approximately 9.9% of them will go straight to Forever27. They don't want to come back down to the drudgery of their usual lives. They have chosen to leave at their peak. Fair enough.

The other 90% will go back to what they were doing, happy they got to experience this one night — one hour, rather — of complete freedom. Perfectly brainwashed to be grateful for the privilege, they will go back to their crappy lives and continue to falsely live in hope for next year's lottery. Forever in vain. All those feel-good campaigns SHIT has been promoting, working its magic on their psyches, keeping them docile.

No one challenging anything it does or says. It has society's best interests at heart, that's what SHIT said. Of course it did.

The remaining 0.1% are the prize winners. Those who won endless steps are the most excited you could possibly ever see someone. If they could burst, they would. They start behaving oddly, running around in circles, jumping up and down, and generally making a mess of themselves through excitement. Some embarrass themselves, giddy with the power of moving however they wish. Last year, Nate Overnewton, an over-excited winner (and huge jerk) climbed up a light tower with the intention of dropping below into the crowd for crowd surfing. Unfortunately for the little show-off, no one cared or even noticed him up there. He threw himself off, plunging into the trampled, compacted ground below. Snapped his neck in an L shape. What a waste of a great prize.

The sex winners are also very excited. They had sex!!! They can now cross it off their bucket list. And some got off on the fact they created a new person to add to this shithole of a city. Sunshine City...please!

Of course, this was just a SHIT research estimate. No one there knew about tonight's plan to blow up the stadium. No one except for the goons, John Sweeney, and Turquoise Fitzenberger, the mayor of Sunshine City and president of the SHIT committee. Statistics are fine if you have a future.

For a small time, the newly formed gang of four allow themselves a dance to blend in with the crowd while still keeping a lookout for John, Boss, and Angel. There is a good chance they could all die tonight so they take this moment to throw caution to the wind. Elio is going off! He finally has friends to show off his Irish dancing skills to. They all circle around him and clap in amazement at his speedy yet on pointe footwork. Michael Flatley would have claimed him as his own son. Aksel's height advantage over the others tasked him with constantly scanning over the crowds for any sign of John, Boss, and Angel.

Then Aksel sees him. Big John Sweeney by the stage stairs.

He doesn't seem to be doing much, just standing there, looking over everyone dancing. He isn't dancing, isn't smiling. He is very hard to read. His face steely with indifference. Aksel has to warn him that the goons are coming his way. Warn him about Turquoise stitching him up, using him.

'There's John. Let's go tell him everything before Boss and Angel get to him.' Aksel points to the lone figure by the stage stairs. They all start to move towards Big John, letting Aksel lead the way.

As they get closer, John's eyes lock onto them as he realises these four are making a beeline for him. He has no idea who they are in their costumes. He takes a few steps backwards, wary, starting to feel like a trapped animal. His fight-or-flight response triggered.

'John, it's me, Aksel.' He lifts his mask. The others back off a bit, giving him some space. 'John, I need to talk to you. It's very important, your life is in danger.' He looks about. 'But not here, someone is looking for you. Please...come into the crowd.' Aksel uses a soft approach. It works. John allows himself to be led in.

'Kay, Ax, wassem up?' John is clearly inconvenienced by them but is also patient with them.

'I heard Ms Fitzenberger talking to some bad men earlier in the corridor,' Aksel begins, 'and your name came up.' He looks John in the eyes. 'I know you've been working for her, John, and I'm not judging you on that, but she is planning on stitching you up.' John starts to turn back. 'Listen to me, John. You're not going to get on the committee, you may not even get out of here tonight.'

John gets defensive. 'Yessum, she tol' me I am winnin'. Gotta wait ova ther' for me prize.' He points back over to the stairs. Takes a step back towards them. Aksel puts his hand on John's shoulder.

'Please listen.' He gets John's attention with some hard facts. 'I know you've put explosives around the stadium and Ms

Fitzenberger wants to blow everyone up tonight. Right?' John hesitates before nodding in confirmation. 'And in exchange she promised you a seat on the committee, right?' John nods in agreement. Aksel puts both hands on his shoulders now and looks him straight in the eye. He's trying to be as genuinely sincere as he can, so John understands. 'She's not going to give you the committee seat, John...she's given it to someone else already.' John seems confused, his eyebrows furrowing.

'But I did for 'er? An' she promise.'

'But Ms Fitzenberger is not a nice lady. She's a liar.' Aksel explains, 'You cannot trust her, John. She has given the committee prize to someone else. Someone bad, and he is also looking for you right now.'

'But why he lookin' me?' John is still putting the scenario together in his head. Aksel is straight.

'Because, John, they are going to kill you. Ms Fitzenberger told them to take care of you tonight after you'd done the explosives.' Aksel re-iterates, 'His name is Boss and he is going to make sure you never leave the stadium tonight. He works for Ms Fitzenberger.' The penny is dropping for John now. 'Ms Fitzenberger gave Boss your prize. He is on the committee now. So, they need to get rid of you.' Aksel stares at John, hoping he finally gets it.

'Dead men tell no secrets, John.'

John is quiet, in thought. 'Huh. OK, Ax.' Unsure if John believes him, Aksel tries another way.

'Have I ever been mean to you, John? Have I ever lied to you?' John shakes his head no. 'Please, you need to trust me on...' Aksel trails off. Something has caught his eye over by the stage steps.

'Is that...?' Everyone follows his gaze to land on two dancers awkwardly standing near the stage, looking very uncomfortable. They are not dancing or smiling. They are both scanning the crowd, serious expressions on their faces like their G-strings are three sizes too small. They look unnaturally rigid in their carnival outfits, like they have been starch ironed into them. To Aksel, they might as well have flashing neon signs above their heads that say 'Goons over here' with arrows pointing at them. Aksel has a knack for seeing through bullshit, he put that gift down to his intelligent parentage. He gets John's attention.

'Look, John, that's them now.' He pushes John into the middle of their circle and tightens it up around him to hide him. Sarita can't help herself; she starts laughing.

'Are these guys serious? They have probably never danced in their whole life.' She guffaws. 'I've seen more relaxed animals before slaughter.' Everyone looks at her like that is a weird thing to say. 'It's a commune thing,' she explains. The explanation is accepted by all.

John is looking over at the two suss goon dancers, his eyes burning into them, his face turning to anger.

'Imma get 'em guys.' He is more talking to himself, but Aksel can see from the change in his face, tone, and demeanour that John understands what's going on. 'Imma get 'em.'

Boss and Angel are standing by the stairs to the stage. Both of them look out over the heaving dancers. From their view it is as if the stadium itself is alive, breathing in and out as the crowd swells and ebbs en masse. It's dark and smoky. The lights are erratic in their movement and provide very little help for them to see anything in detail. In fact, the strobe makes things worse.

'This is ridiculous. Where is Sweeney?' Boss is losing patience fast.

'Fitzenberger said he would be here waiting. Maybe he's coming.' Angel tries to keep him calm.

'Well, if we don't see him by...' Boss checks his watch '...10:45. We must leave. We will have to deal with him tomorrow. We've got to get back to Derek's, see if that idiot is awake yet...fuck!' He stamps his foot, kicks the stairs. 'Fuck this night. Derek's fucked. We may not even be able to harvest tonight, this whole explosion could be a completely wasted opportunity.' Boss chews his lower lip, thinking. 'John's missing. He's the least of our problems right now. Fitzenberger has fucked off and dropped this problem on our heads. I'm not fucking happy.' The part about Turquoise is said with malice. Angel isn't happy either. There's really nothing in this for him to look forward to, all he gets is retaining the niche job as Boss' right-hand man when Boss is on the SHIT committee. This whole situation is a real pain in his arse.

'Fuck her and John. Maybe we keep John for later? Get him to get rid of Fitzenberger. Let's go, Boss. We got bigger shit to deal with. This place is going to blow in 25 minutes.' Angel wants out of the stadium right now.

'This was never part of the original plan. Fuck Fitzenberger, dropping us in her mess like this. We'll give it another five, then we'll go.' Boss' anger has simmered down a fraction upon hearing Angel is thinking the same way as him. He is starting to regret ever associating with Turquoise. She has managed to stitch him up nicely. He imagined working for her on the SHIT committee would be much the same as tonight. Following her around, putting out all the spotfires she lights along the way. Never being able to trust her. This was not one of his finest decisions.

Big John Sweeney is still protected by the salsa-costumed bodyguards encircling him. The crowd still heaves, oblivious to the danger ahead. The music still throbs. The clock is still ticking. Time is running out. The four keep their eyes on the goons. They can tell by their body language Boss and Angel are becoming more frustrated and impatient. They notice Boss kicking the stairs.

'They should be just about ready to get out of here,' Aksel

says of the goons, 'and we should too.' It's said to everyone, including John. They are all thinking it, but Sarita says it first.

'What about everyone else? We can't just leave without trying to warn everyone.' With that, Sarita turns around and heads towards the stage. Elio is worried.

'Wait, Sarita. Where are you going? You're not going to Boss, are you? What about your steps? He's not worth it.' Elio is not keen on her leaving alone. She turns back to him.

'I can't just do nothing. I'm going to get on the stage and tell everyone to leave. The microphones are still there.' She looks frantic. Elio grabs her wrist.

'It's too risky, c'mon. We got to go.' She snatches her wrist away and glares at him.

'No. Where I'm from, we help each other. I have to try.' Her determination can't be denied. Elio knows this.

'Fine then, I'm coming with you.' He turns to the others. 'Stay here and cover John. We'll be back. Maybe you should guys should go to the exit. Soon everyone will be rushing for it.' He swallows back fear. 'Don't get caught in the crush. If we get separated, let's meet at the bridge in the park.'

He takes a second to look at them individually. 'Good luck.'

On that, he turns to follow Sarita's retreating figure. Agnes is keen to get going.

'I'm ready, let's get out of here.' She grabs Aksel's arm and looks to John. 'Ready, John? Let's go.'

'Imma stay an 'ere.' Big John is watching Elio and Sarita as they approach the stairs to the stage. He's watching the goons watching them approach. He talks to Agnes, never taking his eyes off Elio and Sarita, who resume their dancing personas as they approach the stairs. 'Imma help 'em out.' It's said with resolve. Aksel and Agnes know there is no chance of changing his mind and know he is Elio and Sarita's best chance to get out of the stadium.

'Alright, Agnes. Let's go. You want to roll or walk?' Aksel, always courteous. She checks her SLT. Weighs up the risks.

'Think I'll walk till I'm outside, then I'll probably roll.' Agnes is a bit concerned. She just keeps using more and more steps today. She would have to counter-factor them into next week's tally of steps to get her back on track. Aksel looks at Big John, who is still fixated on Elio, Sarita, and the goons.

'Are you...' he's abruptly cut off by Big John.

'You go! Now!' He pushes Aksel in the chest, making him lose balance and step back. Not enough force to hurt him, but enough to send the message he's not fucking around. Aksel instinctively puts his hand in the air in a show of compliance.

'Alright, mate...alright. We're going.' He grabs Agnes' arm. 'Hang on tight, don't want to lose you in the crowd.' Agnes unrolls her jacket and puts it back on; she's going to need it once she's out the gate. They leave for the exit, Aksel leading the way. Big John doesn't look at them as they leave, he's still fixated on the trouble brewing by the stairs.

'What's coming our way, I wonder?' Boss is speaking without even moving his lips. 'They look familiar.' Elio and Sarita are only a few steps away from them now.

'I think we saw them in the corridors earlier, Boss,' Angel observes, 'the dancers.'

'Why aren't they on stage already?' Boss is suspicious of their behaviour tonight.

Boss and Angel are positioned so their bodies block the entrance to the stage stairs, like a couple of bouncers. Elio and Sarita arrive to get onto the stage. Sarita speaks for them; they know Elio's voice.

'Scusi, we just need to get to the stage.' She's trying to sound light and carefree. Neither Boss nor Angel moves. In fact, they don't seem to acknowledge them at all except for a deathly stare.

'Ah hello? May we get past please.' Sarita tries again.

'Why aren't you up there yet?' Boss is quick with his

return this time. Elio and Sarita are caught off guard. They look to each other. Look back at Boss and Angel dressed in their ridiculous attire.

'Why aren't you up there yet?' Sarita turns the question back on them. Boss and Angel have forgotten about the silly dress-ups they have on, and they both look down at themselves. Pointing out their costumes has definitely put Boss offside. His lips curl and eyes narrow. He feels humiliated wearing it. He too had a G-string on. It was turquoise in colour.

Elio elbows Sarita, a warning to rein it in. He knows these guys will swat her like a fly without a second thought if she pisses them off enough. And she's on the right track.

'We're security, bitch. Now piss off.' Boss flicks his head towards the crowd. Angel looks at his watch. He's hyperaware the clock is ticking and they need to get out and get to Derek's.

'Twenty minutes, Boss.' There's no need for Angel to explain further, they both know what it means. They just don't realise the dancers standing before them also know. Sarita and Elio try not to react but can't help grabbing each other's hands. It's noted by Boss and Angel.

As Sarita asks to get to the stage again, she tries to grab the stair rail and push herself around Angel.

'Please. We just need to get to the...' She doesn't get it out as she is violently pushed in the chest, sending her falling backwards onto her bum.

'Ahh! Ow! Why did you do that?!' She has fallen hard on her coccyx and is writhing in pain. This triggers Elio, staying silent now forgotten.

'Sarita! Sarita!' He bends down to her. 'Are you OK?' He touches her face, can see the pain in her eyes. His anger now swells inside like a tsunami about to hit shoreline. He spins to face the goons.

'Fuck you, motherfuckers!' He lashes out to take a swing at

Angel. Misses. Momentum sends him into a spin. Boss knows that voice.

'Welcome back, Elio, you little fuckwit. Where've you been?'

From the crowd, Big John has worked his way close to the stage, never taking his eyes off the goons and his new friends. They protected him. They saved him. Now he has to help them. Even at the cost of his own life. But he isn't as stupid as everyone thinks. Once he sees them all talking at the stage stairs, he quickly makes his way to underneath the stage, staying out of their sight. He can see their lower legs through the gaps in the steps as he tries to overhear what is being said. When Angel pushes Sarita over, he is right under them. He knows she is in pain and struggling to get up. When Elio takes a swing, and he becomes known to Boss, John knows he has to do something immediately. He reaches his strong, sack-dragging arm through the gap in the stairs to grab Angel's ankle. He chooses Angel first because he hurt the pretty lady. Big John Sweeney grabs Angel's ankle and yanks it back as hard as he can, trying to pull him through the gap in the stairs. Angel crashes forwards, narrowly missing Sarita, landing on his face on the concrete. Blood explodes from somewhere underneath his head.

'Run! Run!' John shouts through the stair gaps, telling Elio to leave. 'I got 'er!, I got 'er!' Elio knows John won't leave her alone.

Boss is taken off guard by Angel's quick descent into the cement. For a couple of seconds he has no idea what is happening. That's a couple of seconds more than Angel had. He is out cold. Boss looks to Angel, down at Sarita, back to Angel, to the mysteriously dangerous stairs, back to Angel, then to Elio as he is running away.

'Fuck! Fuck!' He's unsure what to do. Check Angel? Get Sarita? Find out who's under the stairs? Or chase Elio? He decides to chase Elio. He may still be able to help with the harvesting if Derek's not awake. And right now, Elio is making him the most upset. He takes off after him as Elio disappears into the crowd.

Angel is not moving and looks like he will not be going anywhere soon. Sarita is writhing in pain. With adrenalin working for her, she rolls on her side and manages to get on her feet. She takes a couple of painful, pinchy steps, bent over like a centenarian. Before Sarita knows what is going on, she is scooped up by John and thrown onto his back. John purposefully steps on Angel as he leaves, making his way to the exit with his precious cargo.

Elio is running towards the exit, trying to lose Boss, zigzagging through the throng of dancers. It is proving to be harder than he thought, Boss' eyes like heat-seeking missiles honed in on him. Boss curses leaving his gun with Cherub, the useless fuck. He gets held up chasing Elio by a gaggle of dancers whom he can't seem to get past. They push him into the middle of their dance circle and start spinning around him. Eager to enjoy their last 15 minutes of free dance they are working themselves into an intoxicating frenzy. Boss feels someone gyrating on his G-string from behind, grabbing him around the hips and really giving it to him. He is sure he can feel a penile erection poking his arse and spins around quickly to see horny Norman Fitzenberger dry rooting him. Boss snaps, reaching out his arm to grab horny Norman around the neck. He lifts horny Norman off the ground via his neck and punches him in the face with his free hand. Thrice. Horny Norman falls limp and Boss tosses him to the ground like the piece of trash that he is. Puts the boot in for good measure and his own satisfaction. How dare he sexually assault Boss like that.

Finished with horny Norman, Boss looks back up, scanning the crowd for Elio. He cannot see Elio anywhere. He has managed to successfully escape his clutches yet again. Boss is at the end of any patience he ever had. Throws his head back and yells the loudest he can possibly manage. It's long and drawn out. Like an animal in a trap trying to escape.

'Fuuuccccckkkk! Fuck!' He releases some of his frustration. Takes it out on poor horny Norman, repeatedly kicking him in the ribs. He takes a moment to get himself together, re-evaluate his plan. Boss looks back towards the stage steps and sees Angel on his hands and knees, trying to pick himself up off the cement. Boss can't tell from this far away in the dark, but Angel's face is a mess, blood generously flowing, soaking into his collar. Boss watches his crippled form struggling and debates going to help him but decides that him getting his own arse out alive is the better option. He checks his watch. Ten minutes till the explosion. He takes one look back at Angel staggering around and he takes off, self-preservation more important right now. He does hope Angel will make it; he likes him. Angel is the most reliable goon he's ever had by his side, alas there is no time for nostalgia. Boss leaves, heading to Derek's in the hope the fat fuck is finally awake. However, he reminds himself that he left Cherub there also. And Cherub has his gun. He could be walking into anything.

Aksel and Agnes are hurrying their way to the bridge. Aksel is striding hard while Agnes has resumed rolling, probably the fastest she ever has, like she is being blown down the street by a non-existent windstorm. Aside from the distant thump of bass from the stadium, it's eerily quiet, adding to an overall sense of dread. With everybody at the stadium, the city has the feeling of a ghost town. Even though no one is around they stick to the darker fringes of the streets, knowing full well the threat of Boss and Angel on their way to Derek's could be around any corner. They are both concerned and unsure about the fate of their newfound friends. They both really hope they managed to escape unscathed. Aksel's logical brain had figured Sarita and Elio never got far enough to alert everyone at the stadium to leave, or the streets would now be flooded with confused people wondering what the hell was going on. He keeps this fear to himself.

Elio runs straight out the stadium exit and ducks in behind some rubbish skips. His heart is pounding hard as he keeps his eyes on the gates, waiting for Boss, who was hot on his heels, to exit the stadium. He is surprised after he waits for more than a minute and still no Boss. He checks his watch. Not long now. He starts to wonder if Boss went back to get Sarita or Big John. He debates going back in for a few seconds, but he knows it must be less than 10 minutes until the stadium blows. Thoughts of Sarita tear him apart as he is trapped in limbo of what to do next. Just before he can make a decision, Boss comes tearing out of the stadium. Boss stops, does a quick head swivel, no doubt looking for Elio, then takes off in the direction of Derek's. Elio notes that he is alone, no Angel in tow. He quietly thanks Big John, he must have done a real doozy on Angel. Just as he is about to re-enter, Big John exits with Sarita on his back. This sight is the best thing Elio has seen for a long time. He rushes out from the cover of the bins to meet them.

John sees Elio running towards them and gently lowers Sarita down onto the ground. For a rough gem, John could be surprisingly gentle with precious cargo. John pushes hair back from Sarita's eyes and asks her if she is OK just as Elio pulls up beside them. She nods, gives John a grim smile.

'I am now, thanks to you, John.' Sarita looks him in the eye and is sure John is blushing. No one has ever spoken to him with such gratitude, he isn't sure how to handle it. John picks up one of each of Sarita and Elio's hands and links them together.

'You go now.' He looks from Sarita to Elio. 'You go now, danger 'ere.'

'What are you going to do, John? You can't go back in there.' Sarita tries to save her saviour.

'Come with us, John.' Elio reaches his arm out for John to join them, but he swats it away.

'I said you go now. Go!' His voice is getting louder as he becomes increasingly frustrated with them not leaving. Elio and Sarita get the message and start backing off.

'We are all meeting on the bridge in the park, please... come afterwards.' Sarita gives one last try with John. Elio is saddened, feeling like he will never see John again. He doesn't even know him but John has been kind helping them tonight.

'Goodbye, John. And thank you. We will see you soon.' Without further hesitation they both turn and leave, starting their journey towards the park bridge.

Big John Sweeney turns around and heads back into ground zero. Since being stitched up by Turquoise he has decided to return to help evacuate the stadium. Fuck her. And he knows something no one else knows. Because Big John is a whole lot smarter than people give him credit for. The thing is, he never intended to blow up the whole stadium. The plasticine Aksel noticed in his bag was just that. Plasticine. He knew bitchface Fitzenberger would be coming to check on him, so he had to appear as though he were laying explosives. However, he did place real explosives underneath the stage. Bitchface Fitzenberger was meant to be there, wrapping up the night. He had every intention of blowing her up for sure. Yes, there would be some collateral damage, but it would be worth the sacrifice to rid the world of this vile human being. But now, the game has changed. Turquoise Fitzenberger had no intention of being there and is long gone. The only people going to die would be innocent. John's heart felt heavy, he did not feel good about this. As he re-enters, he tells everyone he passes to get out now. They don't pay him much mind until he tells them there is a bomb. Combined with his insistent face etched with anxiety and his imposing presence, people start to believe him. Some start to leave but there is no urgency.

The music stops. The free dance is over. John knows there are three minutes on the timer now, enough time for Fitzenberger to have settled into her goodnight wrap-up. Bitch.

'I'm gonna get 'er,' he mumbles to himself before taking a deep breath in.

Well trained, the crowd have all stopped dancing, fully aware that their steps are back on the clock. Everyone is confused, looking around; nothing seems to be happening. The stadium has dropped from a loud, vivacious banging party to a crowd of disillusioned still people, looking about in silence, in about 30 seconds. A loud commanding voice snaps them all out of their trance as they all turn their heads at once towards the sound. It's Big John Sweeney.

'Is a bomb! Leave now!' He's screaming as loud as he can, using this opportunity of silence to alert everyone. 'Go now. S'not a joke! A bomb! Go!' Not everyone can hear him but the message is soon whispered throughout the crowd and people are now becoming scared. There is a lot of movement as people become restless, still unsure what to do.

Suddenly, screaming can be heard in the back of the stadium, something is coming towards the exit fast. More screaming, cries of pain, coming closer with the large, dark object seemingly bounding its way through the crowd. As it gets closer, John recognises it as a cluster of pogo punks. They'd seemed one entity from a distance, clumping together in a group, but now he can see that clump is made up of around 150 punks. *Thack...boiing. Thack...boiing.* More screaming and cries of pain. The pogo punks are making a break for the exit. Carelessly and selfishly, they bound over the tops of everyone without thought to their potential injuries. Breaking necks, breaking arms, shoulders, and faces just as they had during their entrance, but more frantic this time. This sends the already skittish crowd into a mass panic, and they all start to run/roll/stilt walk/ball/skate/gyro/glide/pole vault/whatever their way to the exit as the pogo punks continue to crash down on them. It's suddenly bedlam. Each to their own.

BOOM!

The stage blows up as the punks pass by. Pogo punks are left hurtling through the air sideways, smacking hard into stadium seating and the ground. Bodies fly into the air like disjointed mannequins, limbs moving independently from their bodies. Their pogos fly off in every direction, causing even more injuries and havoc. Two ballers shoot off into the night somewhere, bouncing off the stadium roof only to disappear out of sight into the night sky.

Elio and Sarita are running as fast as they can to get as much distance from the stadium as possible. Sarita's unknown remaining steps forgotten about in this moment. Running with the stadium behind them they don't directly see the flash, but they both notice the night sky turn to amber and a second later the sound catches up with them.

BOOM!

Elio and Sarita both fall forwards, breaking their fall with their hands, elbows, and knees, crashing into the ground. It isn't a shock wave that pushes them over; running at full speed it scares the hell out of them, catching them off guard.

'Ahhh! No!' Sarita screams out in frustration and sadness. 'No...no.' Her speech makes an unusual sound as it turns to sobbing. She pushes herself off the ground and sits on her bum. She uses her hand to wipe tears from her eyes. Anguish is written across her face as Elio turns his head to face her. He can't bear to see her distraught but knows there is nothing he can do.

Elio rolls onto his back and levers his torso up with his arms, resting on his hands. He isn't sure if his eardrums have burst, it is deathly quiet now post-boom. Sarita's quiet sobbing and distant screaming slowly ebbs into his psyche, and he realises that it is not the case. They both sit for a minute in shock, not talking. Elio looking at Sarita, Sarita looking at the glow in the sky above the stadium. Both of their chests heaving violently from the run and shock. Sarita holds her hand out to Elio. It's shaking. He takes it lovingly and squeezes it tight.

'Are you OK?' Elio looks her in the eyes. Her sobbing has slowed and her face is streaked with snot and tears. Sarita can't muster a verbal response; she nods very slowly. Pulls her legs up to her chest and wraps her arms around them. Making herself as small as possible. Elio shuffles over on the grass and sits beside her, wrapping his arms protectively around her. He gives her a sweet kiss on the cheek.

'All the people, Elio.' She's getting choked up. 'They didn't deserve it. They didn't have to die.' She only just manages to get it out without completely sobbing. 'What about...where is...do you think John made it?' Her brow furrows with genuine concern. He saved her at the stairs and now she's grown quite fond of him.

Elio is unsure what to say to comfort her.

'I think John went back to try and save them.' He thinks for a moment. 'I think he would have saved some people and I think he's going to be OK.' He doesn't really know if what he says is true, but it seems to help Sarita. She dries her eyes off on her sleeve and clears her throat, resolved to seeing this night through.

'Come on.' She looks at Elio, all business now. 'Let's get to the bridge before Agnes and Aksel think we've been blown up too.'

Elio gets up first, steadies himself. Reaches his arm out to help up Sarita, who gratefully accepts. He's silently impressed by her tenacity and ability to cope in seemingly impossible positions.

Agnes and Aksel are on the bridge now, waiting for their friends. They both flinch and duck involuntarily as the night sky lights up amber above the stadium in the distance. Both of their eyes reflect the amber flash of fire. It's not long until the sound catches up.

BOOM!

They both look at each other, not saying a word but each thinking the same thing. No one wants to say it in case it is true, it would be too much. Tears collect in Agnes' eyes, too much to be held in, they make their way down her face. She looks at Aksel, notices his Adam's apple moving up and down as he swallows his emotions. She can see the amber glow in his eyes as he looks to the stadium. Agnes can't hold in her emotions anymore and starts sobbing. The whole day is starting to take its toll. Aksel moves to comfort her, himself on the edge, trying to be brave for his new little sister, Agnes.

'Where's Elio and Sarita?' Agnes manages to string a small sentence together in between sobs. 'Why aren't they here yet?' She looks up to the night sky, places her hands in a prayer position under her chin. 'If there is any higher power up there, please...please bring them back. Please. I'm begging you.' Defeated, she lowers herself onto her bum and sits down. Aksel joins her sitting on the bridge.

'We'll wait here as long as we need to. They'll turn up.' He looks up to the night sky. 'I'm sure they're going to be OK. They'll be here soon.' He doesn't know if he even believes what came out of his own mouth, but it's the only bit of hope they have left right now, and he isn't ready to give it up.

Screaming, wailing, crying, pushing. The crowd in the stadium is in a manic panic. Everyone is rushing for the exit. Each doing whatever they need to get out.

Of course, Turquoise Fitzenberger had pre-arranged for all the gates but one to be locked tonight, making it hard for any potential survivors to escape her planned annihilation. She was relying on Boss and Angel to lock the last gate on their way out after they'd dealt with Big John Sweeney.

Right now, she is safe and sound, snug as a bug in a rug at home. Confident in her cockiness. She's set the mood of victory, playing her beloved musical triptych Carmina Burana by Carl Orff on her record player. It is so rousing and passionate. She feels a connection to the lament about the inescapable power of fate. O Fortuna! She knows the 24 poems by heart and feels she can relate to every single one of them.

Turquoise has succumbed to a few shandies already, a Baileys on ice now sits on her coffee table, condensation pooling around the bottom of the glass. She can see the stadium from her living room window but chooses to pay it no mind. In fact, she is laid out on the sofa in her turquoise-coloured bath robe, charcoal face mask on with slices of pineapples over her eyes. Apparently, the bromelain enzymes in the pineapple flesh work wonders on her puffy eyes. She will tell you it's been used for centuries in Central and South America to reduce inflammation. Turquoise must look the best she can for tomorrow, it's going to be a big day. Press conferences, news coverage, interviews, the list goes on and on. When the bigger part of a city's population dies in a tragedy in one day there's bound to be a lot of hoo-ha, la-di-da about it. It is her time to shine on an international scale. The whole world will be watching as she expresses her well-rehearsed sorrow and sadness for such a tragic event. She'll talk about how she personally saw how happy everyone was in the moments before she had to leave for a 'personal emergency'. How they lived their last moments happy and free and that's all you could want for them. Boo-hoo, boo-hoo, and all that crap. Then weeks later, after everyone has had time to digest the tragedy, rope them into the idea of her being a pioneer of sorts.

Tell them about her plan for a bigger, bolder, more intelligent, exclusive, and elite city.

So back on the sofa, Turquoise is getting a bit of rest and recovery. After all, she did get stampeded and wedgie-d today, so she is feeling a little fraught and frail. She lies still, softly rehearsing her speeches to herself. From the sofa she hears the boom from the stage bomb, her thin wrinkly lips curling at the ends into a clown-like smile. Thinking this means her plan has come to fruition, it gives her a spark like lightning and she gets large goosebumps all over. She shakes them out and continues with her rehearsal.

Everyone trapped in the stadium continues with their struggle. It's now absolute pandemonium. The rush to one exit has created a bottleneck, the one unlocked gate jammed with competing ballers trying to get out first, blocking it off for everyone else. No one is willing to give an inch that isn't going forwards. People are climbing over people, climbing over parts of people, climbing over people that are climbing over people. The pole vaulters are the winners now. They all just casually vault their way over the fencing. The stiltwalkers see this and try to follow suit. They can't walk over the fencing, but they adapt their stilts as pole vaults, hurtling themselves over the fence rather ungracefully.

People are banging on the ballers' balls and trying to man-handle them out of the way but there is nowhere to go. It is jam packed and no one will take a step backwards, even for the greater good of everyone. The ballers are absolutely terrified, trapped in their own clear prisons they can see everyone's anger directed towards them. Some are having panic attacks in their balls, unable to move. Someone else isn't moving at all, slumped lifeless in the bottom of their ball. The noise is a hell soundscape filled with pain and panic. Something the devil might have for a door chime.

One of the gyro boys is circling overheard, dipping down to pick up one person at a time then dropping them over the fence. He is doing well; he is on his ninth descent to pick up when he becomes swamped by people. He tries to take the gyro back up, but people jump up, grasping onto the receding wheels. Then people grab those people until it's too much for the gyro. It comes crashing down on top of those who were pulling it, its blades slicing through some of them before finally stopping rotating once they contact the earth with a sickening thud. The smell of blood and fear emanating from the crash site spreads like liquid poured on the ground.

New loud popping noises start coming from the direction of the exit. Somebody has a rather large knife, similar to one you might see hunters use. In order to unblock the exit, everyone has collectively agreed to sacrifice the ballers by popping their balls while they are still trapped inside. Unfortunately for the ballers, this is like being put in a big plastic bag. The deflated ball sticks to their sweaty skin and forms a plastic cocoon, effectively suffocating the person inside. Stupid ballers, if only they'd been more courteous and allowed people to get through it would not have come to this. Oh well. The plastic cocoon coffins are quickly dragged out of the way and people finally begin to stream out of the stadium. Those who are still able to, that is. Many are now dead, dying, injured, or missing body parts. The smell of fear, explosives, and smoke lingers over the stadium like a toxic raincloud.

Never in his life has Boss ever been so pissed off. Never have his plans gone so awry. The simmering anger inside him is about to reach boiling point. There is so much going wrong. His incompetent assistants. Being dropped in it by Turquoise. Derek not being able to wake up. And horny Norman Fitzenberger really got on his nerves, sexually assaulting him like that. His blood pressure seems to keep escalating. If he cut himself, his blood would spurt out at the rate of a high-pressure fire hose.

He stands in the doorway at Derek's, surveying the room. Nothing has changed except Cherub is now asleep, gun in hand pointed at Derek. With his eyes still pushed in it is hard to tell if he is sleeping or not. Dried blood cakes his face and he is clutching his missing teeth in his other hand. Perhaps he thought he could still get them put back in. Cherub is going to need more than teeth to get his face back.

'Useless fuck.' Talking to himself, Boss spits the words out like he's just sucked the poison out of someone's snake bite. He looks at Cherub with disdain.

Derek is still gurgling away, unmoved since Boss left. The place is still rancid. There are still blood, piss, and faeces aromas heavily lingering in the thick air. The weapon de jour is now on the kitchen table, who knows what happened to the vibrator in his absence. Boss makes a mental note not to touch it. He knows Cherub is a sex-crazed deviant. To be honest, he is pleasantly surprised not to find Cherub abusing an unconscious Derek with it on his return. The window is still open, allowing a trickle of fresh air, nowhere near enough to freshen the place up.

Clearly, there is no chance of harvesting any steps tonight. Everything is fucked.

'Fuck this. I'm going home.' Defeated, Boss steps out the door then turns back to Cherub. 'You can sleep here tonight, Cherub, you little fuck up.' He's had enough for today. He now has early morning plans and he needs to get some rest.

Waiting on the bridge, Agnes and Aksel are solemn. They don't speak much as the weight of the last 11 hours takes its toll. They are exhausted physically, emotionally, and mentally.

They wait on the bridge in hope their new friends return, it's all they have left to believe in. They'll stay all night if they must. Aksel peers into the darkness looking for a sign, any sign. He sees movement as shadows are displaced further down the park. He stands up, like a meerkat he moves his head left and right trying to get a clearer view.

'Someone's coming.' He's excited yet wary, not knowing exactly who it is yet. There's still a chance it could be Boss and Angel but he's not feeling threatened. As the shadows draw closer, he can make out Elio and Sarita's silhouettes. He alerts Agnes to their approach.

'Agnes...Agnes. They're here!' He points in their direction as his voice raises with anticipation. 'Look...look, Agnes!' If he points any harder he will put holes in the air. Agnes gets up to look.

'Oh my! It is them!' She starts waving frantically and gets a wave back. Momentarily forgetting her step count, Agnes starts jumping up and down on the spot, she's ecstatic. 'They made it, they made it, they made it! Woohoo!'

The rollercoaster of emotions is non-stop, she's back on a high as Elio and Sarita finally reach them. Sarita is walking stiffly, rubbing her coccyx. It's hugs all round. They all look at each other in disbelief. Shaking their heads. Trying to keep the tears in their ducts. Everyone speaks at once.

'We weren't sure you guys were going to make it.' Aksel gets in first.

'We almost didn't make it.' Elio is exhausted.

'What happened to your back? Are you OK?' Agnes is concerned about Sarita.

'Yeah. You know what? I am OK. I got pushed over by Angel, I'm a bit sore but I am OK.' She allows a small smile as the depth of the night's events sinks in. Sarita nods her head. 'I am OK.'

'What happened to John?' Aksel is concerned about the fate of his now-friend. Sarita proudly answers.

'John saved me.' She looks to Elio. 'He saved us.'

'John saved both Sarita and I from Boss and Angel after she

was pushed over. He was hiding under the stairs and pulled Angel's leg out from underneath him.' Elio giggles a little. 'A real doozy too, he was out to it, there was a lot of blood.' Back to a serious tone now. 'John told me to run while he took care of Sarita. So I took the opportunity to get out while Boss was bamboozled. He had no idea what was going on. You should have seen him, he was looking about like a stunned mullet.'

'John scooped me up and took me out of the stadium, Elio was waiting for me outside,' Sarita interjects.

'What about Boss? Where did he go?' Aksel is curious as to Boss' outcome.

'He chased me through the crowd, but he couldn't get me. One moment he was hot on my heels, I thought I was a goner. Next time I looked around he was gone,' Elio explains. 'Once I got out the gate I hid. After a minute or so, Boss came running out, had a quick look around, and left. I'd assumed he'd gone to Derek's. Then another minute after that John came out carrying Sarita.' He stops to think for a moment. 'Pretty sure Angel was still in there at that stage. But I can't be sure.'

'So, where's John then?' Aksel still hasn't got his answer.

'He went back in.' Elio drops his eyes to the ground as he says it. His heart is heavy. 'He went back in to try to save people. Try to get them out…That's the last we saw of him.'

They all look at each other, saddened, but still holding a little hope he made it out. Sarita speaks first.

'Well, I guess we stay here tonight and hope he makes it.' She won't give up on her saviour or her positivity. 'He could still be helping people. I'm going to stay until the morning.' She's determined, and the rest of the group can already see there is no point trying to change her mind.

'Well that's it. We're all staying here tonight then,' Agnes declares as she looks at Sarita and gives her a small smile of acknowledgement. 'We should all stay together tonight. It's been a rough one.'

Elio puts his arm around Agnes and draws her in. Aksel

uses his long arms to scoop everyone up in a big group hug.

'Well, I guess we settle in for the night.' Aksel breaks away and lies down on the footbridge, his long legs hanging over at the knees, feet almost touching the water. 'Bags the outside.' He puts on a mock hotelier voice. 'Ladies, would you prefer the protection of the middle positions?' The girls giggle at his accent and return the humour, using a mock posh accent.

'Why yes, that would be delightful. Thank you very much, sir.' Agnes lies down next to Aksel and Sarita follows suit, lying next to Agnes. Elio is the only one left standing.

'I'll take this side.' He lies down next to Sarita, the girls safely wedged between Aksel and Elio.

They look up at the stars, their glow somewhat diminished by the orange glow from the stadium. Elio and Sarita are squeezing each other's hands. The heaviness has lifted somewhat now they are all together, safe, and relatively unhurt. But running on adrenalin all day has rendered them too exhausted to stay awake. Quickly, one by one they succumb to the comfort and solace of sleep.

Chapter 15
SUNRISE

The first dappled rays of early morning sunlight are filtering through the trees, sprinkling the park with a dazzling display. The gentle warm breeze pushes through the branches, creating a sequinned shimmy effect, light glimmering and moving gently. Harmonious. The current environment gives nothing away about the events that unfolded the night before. A few birds flutter about, singing a morning tune. It *could* be paradise. There is still storm debris littered through the park but the flooding has subsided. After they'd fallen asleep, others had come during the night also, their sleeping bodies strewn around the park. There are a few other people mobile, getting about dazed and confused.

The warm spot of sun on Agnes' face rouses her from her deep slumber. She blinks herself awake, raising her hand over her face to block it and clear sleep from the corners of her eyes. She turns her head towards a noise. Aksel is snoring. Not a loud, rumbling incoming freight train snore, more of a cute cat enjoying an afternoon nap in the sun snore. She turns her head to look the other way, to Sarita. She's starting to wake up also, stirring. Elio sleeps completely silently, she has to look at his chest and make sure he is still breathing. Agnes hoists herself into sitting position, leaning back on her arms. She takes stock of the park, admiring the natural light show. A small smile forms on her lips. She takes a moment to stretch her arms up and arch her back, taking a deep breath in. Then it hits her.

There are people in the park. There are people in the park! Survivors from the free dance.

'Oh...oh...Aksel.' She starts to shake Aksel's shoulder. 'Aksel, wake up. Sarita, Elio. Look...look. There are people. Alive people.'

Sarita wakes first and props on her elbows, looking over the park.

'Ahh. Stupid back still hurts a bit.' She rolls to the side and rubs her lower back. She whacks Elio in the ribs.

'Elio. Look. Wake up.' She whacks him again. 'Wake up. Look, people from the dance.'

Elio wakes quickly, snapping his eyes open and standing up straight away, like he has an off-and-on switch.

Aksel is now also awake and is looking over the park, smiling.

They did not know about John's plan to only blow up the stage. They were expecting the whole stadium had blown up with everyone inside.

'I...how...didn't the stadium blow up last night?' Aksel is confused, looking at everyone for confirmation that he is not dreaming. 'Look what they're wearing. These people are clearly from the free dance.'

Everyone looks at their own costumes from last night, a reality reminder.

'I'm surprised anyone survived,' Elio agrees, looking around confused. 'There are quite a few people here.'

Everyone takes a moment of silence to take in this one little scene. The light. The people. It is...pleasant. Even with the storm debris.

'I'm going to wash my face, freshen up a bit.' Sarita stands. She's a bit wobbly on her feet, almost falling over, like her body is dizzy. She has a moment to herself, rubbing her back, then walks off the bridge, still struggling with vertigo, she travels downstream 20 metres to a quiet little pond.

Elio watches her closely, noting she seems tired this morning. No surprise really, given the events of the past day. He is still concerned about her step count and hopes she won't go any further.

Aksel takes a moment to check his SLT, see how much damage yesterday did to his step count. 28 997 385 steps remaining. Agnes notices this and does the same. Her tracker now reads 31 000 202. Past her daily quota, she's glad she made the decision to roll once they left the stadium. Both are way over what they would usually use, they look at each other, Agnes chewing her bottom lip and wringing her hands together. They don't need to say anything, the conversation is all in their faces.

Sitting at the edge of the pond, Sarita splashes her face with water then throws her head back, face in the sun, allowing it to warm her. It gives her the most beautiful glow Elio could never muster in a dream. He's intoxicated by her aura, watching her from the bridge as Aksel and Agnes poke fun at each other's hair, but he is oblivious to their skylarking. He has tunnel vision right now.

Agnes is reaching up, trying to tousle Aksel's hair but can barely reach it. She's got the giggles as he tries to evade her, ducking and weaving to avoid her hands.

'Woah! Better luck next time, shorty,' Aksel goads her playfully. Agnes is huffing and puffing, all that movement warming her up. She takes off her coat. As she hangs it over the bridge handrails, she notices the letter she pulled out of the letterbox yesterday morning tucked away snuggly in her waterproof pocket. In the drama of the past 20 hours, she's completely forgotten about it.

'Oh, I'd forgotten about this. Finally, something to look forward to.' She unzips the pocket section and pulls it out.

'What's that?' Aksel is curious.

'Not long before you found me stuck in the bog yesterday morning, I found this letter in a pile of debris.' She looks coy. 'Actually...it was in a letterbox that washed down in the flood.' Aksel raises his eyebrows at her questioningly. She's a touch embarrassed. 'Fine. I have a thing about reading other people's mail. It makes me curious.' She looks down at her feet and continues the confession. 'I've been stealing mail for years.' She's still trying to justify her actions. 'It really is interesting, it gives you an amazing insight into other people's lives.'

'Yeah...yeah. I don't care Agnes. That's probably the worst thing you've ever done in your life.' He tousles her hair cheekily. 'Pretty sure I can overlook that.' Aksel now weirdly finds himself curious about the letter also. 'What's in it? What does it say?'

Throughout all this banter Elio is still quiet, gazing over the park and keeping his eyes on Sarita, who is enjoying some quiet time by the creek. He can tell she wants some time to herself, so even though he wants to go to her, he gives her some space and remains admiring from afar. He has no idea what Agnes and Aksel are talking about, it is just white noise.

Agnes carefully opens the back of the envelope. The way she runs her nail through the seal is ritualistic and well-practised. Her face lights up as she does it. Aksel can see that stealing and reading other people's mail really does it for her. He smiles at her joy. She takes the letter out of the envelope, puts it up to her nose, and smells it, eyes closed. Aksel finds it funny but also a bit weird.

'What...are you doing?' He laughs a little as her eyes snap back open. She explains.

'Sometimes you can smell different things in the paper, the ink. Sometimes the paper is scented.' She offers it up for him to smell. 'I like to imagine where it came from. This envelope is blank so that's even more exciting.' She opens the letter and Aksel drops in behind her to read it over her shoulder. Neither of them reads aloud, just to themselves.

Upon finishing the letter, their jaws slowly drop open in surprise and they look at each other seriously, mouths agape. Their expressions say it all as Aksel talks first, very quietly. More like mouths the word to Agnes.

'John? Big John Sweeney?' They look at each other astounded and shocked. Agnes slowly nodding her head. Their gaze is broken by Elio hollering.

'John, John! Look...Agnes. Aksel. John's coming.' Elio is pointing frantically up the pathway. 'Look over there! He made it!' Elio is becoming more animated as John's figure cuts through the dappled lightplay, heading in their direction.

Aksel and Agnes look up to see him coming. They are very happy to see him but are now like cats on a hot tin roof with the letter open in their hands. Aksel quickly grabs it out of Agnes' hand and hides it in his pocket. They look at each other, they don't need to say it, but it remains unsaid that they will keep this to themselves, for now at least. Aksel walks towards John.

'I'm so happy to see you.' He is genuine in his words, gives John a hug. John is not used to people touching him and he stands rigid like a light post as Agnes and Elio follow, enveloping John in a tsunami of arms. He's never been hugged. He likes it.

'Sarita, look who's here! It's John! John!' Elio calls out to Sarita, she's still down the creek enjoying her time alone. Sarita looks at them and smiles the biggest smile. She gives a big friendly wave to John. Her saviour is safe. She gets up and starts towards them, wobbling, her vertigo still with her. Everyone starts peppering John with questions.

'Are you OK?' Agnes looks him up and down, checking for injuries.

'What happened in there?' Elio wants to fill the gaps.

'I thought the stadium was going to blow up completely.' Aksel is confused.

'There are people, look, survivors.' Agnes points around

the park, backing up Aksel's statement. 'You did it John, you saved them'.

'Where are Boss and Angel?' Elio needs to know if his life is still in jeopardy.

'Yeah, did you get them? Are they still alive?' Aksel is also interested to know their fate.

'Did many people died?' Agnes hopes the casualties were few. Interestingly, by the end of the night, more people were hurt by the actions of their fellow people than the stage explosion.

John is a little overwhelmed by all the attention and questions. He imagines this is what it's like to be a celebrity, everyone wanting a piece of you. All three hanging off his every word, not that he has had the opportunity to talk yet.

'I's only gonna blow th stage anyways, wanto kill Fritzelburg, no one else. I's never gonna blow th whole thin.' Big John finally gets a word in.

'But...I saw you underneath with the bomb-making stuff.' Aksel is confused, 'You were putting it everywhere.'

'Nah, Ax. Just tricks. For Fluzenfritzel.' He always calls Turquoise a different last name, just to show his disrespect and annoy her. He knows very well what her last name is, but it's his little direct insult to her. She thinks she is so important everyone should know her name, and John doesn't play those games. He likes to remind her she is no one. It's the little things.

'Where at Sarita? Howser back?' John is looking around for her. Elio turns back to where she was by the pond area and sees her lying face down on the ground a few steps away from where she'd sat. She's not moving. Suddenly, his heart drops, his fear now on his face. He breaks away from the group and runs to her.

'Sarita! Sarita!' Elio tells himself she's just fallen asleep again, but he knows he's being hopeful. She was excited to see John before, when they caught her attention, she'd already started towards them. Startled by Elio screaming her name, everyone turns to see Elio rushing to her still body and they all quickly follow suit. By the time they get to her, Elio is already clutching her head in his lap, tears streaming down his face. He's trying to resuscitate her, breathing in her mouth and pumping her chest. Begging and crying in between. Trying to negotiate her return to life with the powers that be. Tears and snot streaking his red face. He's blubbering.

'No...Sarita...please...wake up.' He shakes her shoulders, slaps her face lightly. Keeps giving her mouth to mouth. He starts bargaining with her. 'If you wake up now, I promise I will do everything I can for you, I promise. Anything you want. Anything. Please...Sarita...wake up.' He is sobbing now, in between trying to strike a deal with her. Agnes, Aksel, and John are all down on their knees circling Elio and Sarita. Everyone stunned by the instant brutality of her death, no one knows what to say. It's traumatic watching and being a part of this. There is no way to comfort anyone. There is no comfort to be had. Sarita has passed, her steps have finally come to an end. Her body's cells have imploded. There is no going back.

Elio is so distressed there is nothing they can do for him but be there. He starts wailing loudly. They had not known Sarita long but her spunk, carefree attitude, and lust for life had infiltrated everyone she'd met. That commune spirit could not be broken, though it was tested.

'Noooo! Nooo! This isn't fair!' The injustice of it all is hard for Elio to take. Aksel moves around to him and stops his hands from pumping her chest, holds them steady as he looks in Elio's eyes.

'She's gone, Elio.' It's said quietly and respectfully. Aksel gently closes her eyes.

Elio is close to hyperventilating as he starts to accept Sarita is gone. Agnes is sobbing and Aksel and John both have tears in their eyes. John quickly wipes his away, he is ashamed to cry but seeing his new friends emotionally open up like this is moving. This is the first time he has cried since he was a young boy. Not that he is crying...

Before her beauty regime last night, Turquoise had consumed four shandies and two Baileys on ice and fallen into a deep sleep on her sofa. The pineapple slices have dried onto her eyes, those bromelain enzymes now working against her, momentarily sticking them shut. Her record with Carmina Burana finished long ago and is still turning, the needle scratching, waiting to be lifted. Her usually well-coiffured hair is now flattened on the back of her head.

The urgent insistent ringing of her telephone wakes her, reminding her today is her big day. Various media and news reporters have been calling all night, but she was out to it and only just came to. She makes moaning noises as she gets up to answer the phone. She's tired, sore, and hungover. She peels off the stuck pineapple from her eyes, taking some eyelashes and brows with it. She's a bit dazed and gives herself a minute to fully wake up before she answers any calls. Moving to the window, she opens it up to let some fresh air in while rehearsing her speeches again, as she did last night. The morning is glorious and the fresh air feels amazing, she is enjoying it on her face. A natural hangover helper.

She looks towards the stadium, which is now surrounded by emergency crews and carbonisers cleaning up the dead.

'I suppose I better answer my people and freshen up.' She's talking to herself.

Her eyes scan the streets; it now dawns on her that there are a lot more people around than there should be. Her brow furrows in disappointed curiosity. Looking back to the stadium she now realises that most of it is still standing. In fact, she can only see damage around the stage area.

'Why aren't you all dead yet? What...' Her voice trails off

as she notices someone standing on the street, looking up at her window. She freezes, her stomach drops. They sure do not look happy with her.

Boss has been waiting for Fitzenberger to wake up for hours. Patiently waiting on the street outside her house, never taking his eyes off her windows, just waiting for her to see him. He has no plans for her today, he just wants to make her sweat, instil fear into her day. Turn her day of glory into a day of anxiety, always looking over her shoulder. Play with her a bit. Cat and mouse.

He wants her to know he is coming for her. She knows she stitched him up last night and their relationship might sour. But she doesn't really know Boss. She is going to learn more about him, like it or not.

Their eyes lock. Nothing, yet everything is said as Boss holds his steely gaze. He raises his hand, using his index finger to do a cutthroat action under his neck. The international sign for 'I'm going to fuck your shit up'. He wants to make his intentions very clear.

Turquoise almost faints at the sight. Her stomach somersaulting. Her legs suddenly wobbly and weak. She breaks eye contact quickly, unable to hold his gaze.

She backs away from the window and slams it shut, drawing the curtains.

About Atmosphere Press

Founded in 2015, Atmosphere Press was built on the principles of Honesty, Transparency, Professionalism, Kindness, and Making Your Book Awesome. As an ethical and author-friendly hybrid press, we stay true to that founding mission today.

If you're a reader, enter our giveaway for a free book here:

SCAN TO ENTER
BOOK GIVEAWAY

If you're a writer, submit your manuscript for consideration here:

SCAN TO SUBMIT
MANUSCRIPT

And always feel free to visit Atmosphere Press and our authors online at atmospherepress.com. See you there soon!

About the Author

SAM A.D. has spent over 25 years reading other peoples stories and helping them come to life through her film and television career. Now she has her own story to tell in this debut – *Steps*.

Sam A.D. is based in Melbourne, Australia.

Milton Keynes UK
Ingram Content Group UK Ltd.
UKHW040308181024
449757UK00005B/422